"You have every right to be upset about it... Justice hasn't been served."

"Honestly?" She looked up at him with sad eyes. "It's like a book with no ending. Those final chapters are missing where the bad guy gets what's coming to him and everyone can go on with their lives. Start to really heal. I feel so stuck. I can get so far with the process, but then...I hit a wall. Because there's no..." Her voice trailed off and he realized she was on the verge of tears.

"No closure," he said softly. "I understand."

They were quiet for a few moments as Ryan let Andi regain her composure. When she was ready, she dabbed her eyes with her napkin and lifted her head. "Okay. So back to being proactive again. Like you said before, at some point this person is going to make a mistake."

Ryan knew she was right.

He also hoped that the mistake didn't come at her expense. Because there was no way he could let anything happen to her.

Donna Alward lives on Canada's east coast with her family, which includes her husband, a couple of kids, a senior dog and two zany cats. Her heartwarming stories of love, hope and homecoming have been translated into several languages, hit bestseller lists and won awards, but her favorite thing is hearing from readers! When she's not writing, she enjoys reading (of course), knitting, gardening, cooking...and she is a *Masterpiece* addict. You can visit her on the web at donnaalward.com and join her mailing list at donnaalward.com/newsletter.

DANGER
NEXT DOOR

DONNA ALWARD

LOVE INSPIRED
INSPIRATIONAL ROMANCE

LOVE INSPIRED®
INSPIRATIONAL ROMANCE

ISBN-13: 978-1-335-63342-2

Danger Next Door

Copyright © 2021 by Donna Alward

This edition published by arrangement with Harlequin Books S.A.

For questions and comments about the quality of this book, please contact us
at CustomerService@Harlequin.com.

Love Inspired
22 Adelaide St. West, 40th Floor
Toronto, Ontario M5H 4E3, Canada
www.LoveInspired.com

Printed in U.S.A.

Be strong and of a good courage, fear not,
nor be afraid of them: for the Lord thy God,
he it is that doth go with thee;
he will not fail thee, nor forsake thee.
—*Deuteronomy* 31:6

With many thanks to Cindy Renouf—
good friend, kindred spirit and retired
RCMP officer—for helping me with the finer points
in this story. Any liberties taken are entirely mine.

And to Darrell,
for an incredible summer of lockdown and for
bringing me beverages on the deck as I wrote
most of this book in the sunshine. If 2020 was
a test, we passed it with flying colors, baby!

Chapter One

Andi hesitated at the entrance to the woods, steeling herself for the painful walk ahead. She did this every year on this date: September 19. Every year for the last six years, to mark the anniversary of the day she'd lost all hope and her beautiful, perfect life crumbled to dust.

The leaves in the foothills of the Rockies had started to turn, and the forest carpet beneath her feet was covered in gold leafy coins, bright yellow from the poplars and birches already shedding their leaves in preparation for winter. She took a first step, then another, moving forward until her car, parked along the dirt road, was obscured from view. She didn't worry about getting lost. She knew the way well enough by now. Would never forget it. It was etched indelibly on her brain and on her heart. Because seven years ago she'd made this walk with a crime scene as her destination.

Andi's heart was unbearably heavy as she determinedly made her way forward. Birds still sang in the trees, but the sky that had been a piercing blue earlier in the day had given way to dull, gray clouds. Fall used to be her favorite season, but Chelsea's death had tainted the season forever. It was said that mothers never got over losing their children. If that was true, it must be doubly true for mothers whose children were ripped away from them and then murdered. The violence of it was an additional stab of the knife, adding to her grief. She should have protected her little girl. She'd failed her so utterly.

She swallowed thickly against the emotion bubbling up in her throat, but kept moving, always forward. She did this on the anniversary of Chelsea's death because she would never forget the angel she'd been given for three brief but beautiful years. Her marriage had foundered in the months following and ultimately ended in divorce. Grief had nearly consumed her. But on the anniversary of her baby's death, Andi came out here to talk to her daughter and feel close to her. If that made her unhinged, she'd accept it.

Her baby's killer had never been found. He or she was out there somewhere, living their life, while her baby girl had been denied hers, and Andi had worked very hard not to let her anger about it consume her. Her fingers gripped the bouquet of daisies in her hand even tighter. Daisies, because that last summer Chelsea had picked every single one she could find, in yards and ditches and up against fences, presenting them to Andi with a bright smile and twinkling eyes. "Flower," she'd say. "For you, Mama."

Oh, how that memory still hurt, even as Andi kept it tucked away in her heart for safekeeping.

It didn't take long to reach the familiar circle of trees, and she paused, an uneasy feeling settling over her. The birds had gone silent and the air was still, barely ruffling the leaves remaining on the trees. Tall poplars mingled with spruces, forming a perimeter around a small clearing maybe fifty feet in diameter. Her heart was pounding now, not because of any exertion but from emotion and anxiety.

Her baby had been killed here. Choked, strangled, until she stopped breathing and her heart no longer beat. Grief rose, sharp and ruthless, causing a searing pain right beneath Andi's rib cage that stole her breath.

"Chelsea," she whispered, tears clogged in her throat. "I miss you, baby."

A cool breeze came up and fluttered the leaves, the rustling creating an ominous shushing sound in the dismal autumn afternoon. Her pulse quickened. She could do this. She lifted the daisies and took a long inhalation for strength. After another big breath, she stepped forward into the circle and forced herself to look at the tree. The biggest birch, beneath which Search and Rescue had found Chelsea's lifeless body.

The flowers fluttered to the ground in a clump as icy shock raced through Andi's body.

Nailed to the tree was Chelsea's stuffed rabbit—the same one that had gone missing with her the morning she disappeared.

Andi couldn't breathe. Her mind took off in all directions as she stared at the small stuffed animal that her daughter could never be without. It had not been surprising that it had vanished with her. But unlike

Chelsea's body, it had never been found. Until now. And it was nailed to that tree... Deliberately. The nail was rammed in right through the rabbit's neck, its head drooping sideways, ears flopping listlessly.

By the killer? It could be no one else. That knowledge settled around her, chilling her blood. Whoever killed Chelsea had kept that rabbit. And they had brought it back here. Why? A trophy? How sick was that?

"Think, Andi. Think." She spoke quietly to herself, trying to focus. What did she need to know? Do? Not panic. She couldn't panic. Her breaths came sharp and fast, and she braced her hand on the smooth bark of a poplar tree for support, struggling to keep from hyperventilating.

Was the killer nearby? How did he—or she—know that Andi came here each year? Was she in danger right this minute? She took a moment to scan the forest around her, peering into the trees. No sound other than her own breathing. No footsteps of any kind. Just that eerie, dark feeling. Like she was being watched.

Her gaze was drawn back to the bunny on the tree. Everything in her wanted to go to it, pluck it away, keep it close. But common sense prevailed, and she knew she couldn't. Not if there was any chance at all that it could lead to Chelsea's killer.

Her head turned sharply at the snap of a branch somewhere to her right. More sounds, like something—someone—moving quickly. She froze for an instant, shock and adrenaline rippling through her body. Then she took off toward the sound, abandoning all caution in her pursuit. For seven years she had longed to know the identity of her daughter's killer. They wouldn't get away this time, not if she had anything to say about it. Her head told her that to follow would put her in danger. Her heart overruled it, willing to take the risk. She was, in that moment, a mother seeking justice for her child. A terrifying creature indeed.

Her feet crushed the leaves on the forest floor, and she used her arms to shove away branches as she followed the sound deeper into the woods, her heart hammering so loudly she could hear it in her ears. A branch snapped and struck her in the face; she barely registered the sting and kept pushing forward, following the noise.

The crashing came from her left now, and as she pivoted, she caught sight of a mule deer running off, eyes wild with fright as it raced deeper into the forest.

Andi stopped, gasped for breath and let the tears come. It was just a stupid deer! What in the world had she been thinking? Chasing after an animal… What if it had been Chelsea's killer? What would she have done if she'd caught up with them? She was five foot five and had no weapon. Still, for a moment it had felt good to be the one in pursuit. However, now she was alone in the woods, feeling lost and alone and…adrift.

That feeling of being adrift was too familiar and sucked her back into the dark days after Chelsea had gone missing. It had taken Andi a long time to crawl out of that darkness, and she was terrified of going back there again. She needed help. Guidance. As tears stung her eyes, she whispered, "Why? Why now, God?" Hadn't she been through enough? Healing had taken so long, not that one ever got over losing a child. But now, with the appearance of one small toy, the wounds that had been tentatively stitched together were ripped open again. Anger slid, dark and unsettling, through her veins. She looked up at the sky. "How can You be so cruel?"

As quickly as she asked it, a peace settled over her. Expecting divine intervention at this moment was naive, wasn't it? Instead, she looked to herself for what to do next. For starters, she had to calm down and breathe. She'd raced through the forest without any care or attention to where she was going, and the first thing she had to do was get back to the trail. She looked up; the sun was still behind the clouds. Then she turned around and searched for signs of where she'd gone racing through the trees after the deer. A deer, for heaven's sake. She shook her head with disbelief.

She picked her way back carefully, following broken branches and her footprints in the soft earth until she spied the trail. Then she followed it to the clearing again. The stuffed bunny was still there. She let out a sigh of relief. She hadn't imagined it. On impulse, she took out her phone and snapped a picture of it.

She had to call the police, didn't she? This was new evidence. And yet she hesitated. She still remembered the awful hours of being questioned. Remembered the investigator asking if she usually slept and left her child unattended. If she took cold medication a lot. If she ever took anything else. She'd never been able to understand why they kept asking her questions while her baby was out there somewhere, alone and in danger. After all, she'd blamed herself. Having the police suggest she was also at fault only made that heavy feeling worse. She didn't want to call this in. Wasn't ready for that kind of scrutiny again. It had broken something inside her the first time, something that had scabbed over but never fully healed.

But there was one officer she could trust, she realized. Ryan. She'd call Ryan Davenport, her best friend's brother and a corporal at the Cadence Creek RCMP detachment. Throughout the entire investigation he'd been kind and gentle. Of all the officers she knew, she trusted him the most. He'd know what to do next and wouldn't treat her like a criminal.

She checked her cell and let out a huff of irritation. No reception. She was going to have to go back to the car and hope for the best. And that meant leaving the scene right now…and the bunny. She was strangely afraid that if she left, it would disappear, as if she'd imagined it. But what other choice did she have? At least she had the photo.

Her gaze stuck to the rabbit again, so brutally nailed to the tree, ears flopping down, the soft brown fur matted. Chelsea had been attacked just as violently, and for a moment Andi thought she might be sick. It was a bad idea to let those images race around in her head. She swallowed against the bile rising in her throat and deliberately pushed the thoughts aside.

The only choice was to leave the scene so she could make the call. Reluctantly, she started back through the woods to where her car waited, this time with hurried steps and a racing heart but a much clearer head. What did this all mean? Why now? What did the killer want?

"We're going to get you this time," she said roughly, jogging down the narrow trail. The new determination mingled with something that had been missing for a long time—hope. "And you're going to pay for what you did."

Ryan looked at the number on his cell and wondered why in the world Andi Wallace would be calling him. The only other time she'd called him personally was when the Davenport extended family had gone camping for a week in Rocky Mountain House, and his sister, Shelby, had dropped her phone in the bathtub and didn't have a replacement yet. Andi had been cat sitting and Shelby had given Andi Ryan's number as an emergency contact. He and Andi weren't friends, per se. Something twisted in his stomach. If she was calling because something had happened to Shel…

"Hello?"

"Ryan?"

"Andi, is that you?"

"Yeah. Are you on duty?"

"Not today. Just home splitting some wood for winter. What's up?"

"I need a favor."

There was a tremor in her voice, and she sounded out of breath. He put down the ax and furrowed his brow. Something wasn't right.

"What's going on? You sound upset."

"I am. Okay. I don't know how to say this without sounding crazy, so please don't judge. I was out to the crime scene today and I saw something that…" There was the sound of a deep breath, in and out. "Something that wasn't there before. Can you come out here?"

Ryan stilled. She didn't have to say where; he knew the crime scene area as well as anyone. He'd been a rookie, a brand-new addition to the detachment, when her daughter had been murdered. That kind of thing was branded forever on a person's psyche. More so because it was his first homicide scene. A guy didn't forget something like that.

"What did you find, Andi?" He asked the question cautiously, afraid of the answer. It had always bothered him that they'd never caught the killer. He prayed she hadn't found another victim.

"Something of Chelsea's. Please, Ryan... I don't want to call the detachment and get a whole investigation involved if I'm being..."

She stopped, and he knew what she was going to say. *Crazy.* At the time, the investigation had considered her statement of events unreliable. She'd been asleep when Chelsea had disappeared. There was some skepticism that plain old cold medication could have knocked her out so completely.

And then he heard a muffled sniff, and he knew he had to go. He liked Andi. He'd never believed for one moment the theory that she'd somehow been involved. There'd been unanswered questions, yes, but Andi had been the most dedicated and loving young mother he'd ever known.

"I'll be there in fifteen minutes. Can you hold on?"

"My car's parked on the dirt road east of the site. I'll be waiting there. I couldn't get reception in the woods."

"Hang tight, Andi," he said, trying to sound reassuring. "I'll be there as soon as I can."

Ryan grabbed his wallet from inside the house and hopped into his half-ton. Within minutes he was headed out of Cadence Creek and toward the foothills of the Rockies. The dirt road was off the beaten path, though in fairly good shape, with only the odd hunting or summer cabin tucked away in the trees. Ryan reached over to the passenger seat and picked up his bright orange ball cap. Better to be visible in the woods than not. While some species' hunting seasons had yet to open, he knew not everyone followed the rules, and he'd rather be safe.

It didn't take long for him to spy her car, parked over on the narrow shoulder, and he pulled in behind it. She was standing by the hood and moved into the road when he put the truck in Park. Her dark hair was pulled into a ponytail and she wore jeans and a light jacket, suitable for the temperature but not if the showers forecast came to pass. Ryan took a steadying breath as he hopped out and went to her. Andi's face was white as a sheet and her eyes…well, her eyes were haunted. Whatever she'd seen had really given her a start.

"Hey, Andi," he said, trying to sound calm and reassuring.

"Thank you for coming. You were the only one I could think to call."

He nodded. "Of course. But before we go in there, I want you to tell me what you saw." No way was he going in blind. He didn't want any sorts of surprises.

"Right. Okay." Nerves still cluttered her voice. "So

here's the thing. Every year, on the anniversary of her death, I come out here. I know it sounds silly…"

"No, it doesn't. It sounds like grief. Go on."

Her face relaxed a little. "I came out today but…but I'm sure someone else has been there. They left something behind."

His gaze moved from her face to the rest of her body. She stood stiffly, and her hands were shaking. Add that to the frantic quality of her voice and he'd say she was on the verge of a panic attack.

He moved forward and took her hands in his. They were ice-cold and trembling, so he rubbed his thumbs over the tops reassuringly. "It's okay. I'm here. Slow down. Breathe." He modeled nice, even breaths for her until she started to have deeper respirations. Having her hyperventilate wasn't going to help either of them.

Her hands felt small and fragile in his, and his gut twisted. Seven years ago, Andi had been twenty-eight and practically luminescent in motherhood. She'd doted on Chelsea, and the times he'd seen the girl, she'd adored her mother, too. Shelby had been pregnant at the time with her first, and Ryan remembered the two of them, heads together, talking about pregnancy and motherhood. That she'd had something so dear to her torn away still haunted him.

"Better," he reassured her. "Now tell me what you saw."

"Chelsea's stuffed rabbit, the one that went missing with her but was never found."

"What, just lying there?" In seven years, in all her

trips back, she'd never seen it? And how had they missed it when they analyzed the crime scene?

"No, that's just it." Her gaze locked with his. "Ryan, it's nailed to a tree. The tree where she was found." She pulled out her phone and brought up the picture.

A heaviness settled in his stomach as he stared at the photo. It was clearly a stuffed rabbit, but photos could be deceiving, depending on the perspective and angle, and he wanted to get a sense of the whole scene. "I think you'd better show me. Hang on." He jogged back to the truck and came back with an orange vest. "Here, put this on. This time of year, you should be wearing hunter's orange."

She shrugged the vest over her shoulders. It was too big for her, but at least they'd both be visible.

He followed her into the woods, stepping carefully, keeping his eyes peeled for anything or anyone that seemed off or out of place. The sun had gone completely under clouds now, and the air chilled as the light dimmed beneath the tree canopy. He trusted she knew where she was going, so he was happy for her to take point as they made their way deeper into the forest. Keeping sharp was important right now. He couldn't allow himself to go back to the last time he was here. He'd spent enough time doing that in his nightmares.

The murder of Andi's daughter had affected him more than anyone truly knew. But if Andi could face it, so could he.

When they got close to the site, Andi reached back and took his hand. "It's just ahead, in that circle of trees."

He held her hand because she seemed to need the re-assurance. And when they reached the small clearing, acid burned in his throat.

He could still see Chelsea lying there.

His gaze lifted to the bark of the birch tree, where a stuffed animal was nailed to the trunk. He moved a little closer, but not much. He didn't want to risk contaminating a scene with his own footprints.

"You're right. Someone did that deliberately. But it might not be hers, Andi. We can't assume anything."

"It's exactly like hers. She took it everywhere with her."

He let out a slow breath and used his cop brain. "Right. But look at me for a moment."

She did, and he gave her a second to really focus on what he was about to say. "I know it looks like someone took her toy and put it there deliberately, but we can't assume anything, okay? The worst thing we can do is go into a scene with a preconceived notion of what we'll find. We've got to let the evidence lead us, instead of letting us lead the evidence. Do you know what I mean?"

She nodded quickly, but he wasn't sure she really got it. And how could she? She was emotionally involved. For goodness' sake, he was emotionally involved. But he had to do this right. "Andi, we need to call this in, and we need to do it now." He looked up at the sky and the increasing clouds. "If it rains, any evidence might be washed away."

"But you believe me."

"Of course I believe you. I can see it for myself."

To his shock, tears started to trickle down her face. "What's wrong?"

She looked up at him and her lip wobbled. "I needed someone to believe me. I was afraid if I called it in, they'd think I was losing it."

He knew why. When Chelsea had gone missing, Andi had gone through a lot of questioning. She'd had to be ruled out as a suspect. He figured that did a number on her, and it wasn't likely to be something a person forgot. The last thing she needed was for someone to say she'd put the rabbit there herself. And he believed her 100 percent. Always had.

"You're not losing it. And we can't even say these are connected, but the coincidences are enough that it warrants investigation, okay? Let's go where we can get a signal and I'll call it in."

She nodded, then reached for his hand. "For seven years I've wanted to find the person who took my daughter from me. If this can reopen the case…"

"One step at a time," he said softly, squeezing her fingers. But deep down he knew she was right. This one thing might be all it took to reopen Chelsea's case. And then maybe that precious little girl would get the justice she deserved.

Chapter Two

Andi was so thankful for Ryan. He stayed with her as other officers from the detachment arrived and began to process the scene—setting up a perimeter, marking evidence, taking photographs. When she was asked questions, he stood at her side. He answered the questions directed at him. But when it came to the scene itself, he stood back. "In this case, I'm a witness," he explained. "Don't worry, Andi. They know what they're doing."

She turned her gaze up at him, unable to hide the doubtful expression on her face. "I wish I could believe that."

His eyes held hers. "You trust me, and I trust them."

Andi tried not to have doubts, but after seven years with no arrest, her confidence in procedures was shaky. In this moment, she was trying to process what she recognized was trauma. Seeing the yellow tape go up around the perimeter of the scene instantly took her back seven years to the horror of losing her daughter. She told herself it was normal to feel traumatized at this moment. She'd have to unpack it later, work through it. Right now, she was trying to stay anchored and present in the moment. Ryan was that anchor keeping her grounded. She would fall apart later when she dealt with all her feelings.

She was glad she'd taken grief therapy, and thankful for Ryan, who hadn't left her side in the two hours since meeting her on the service road.

"Ma'am, you're free to go. For now." The sergeant in charge addressed her as she stayed outside the yellow tape. She got the implication. She was only in the way. And she didn't want to be. But leaving was hard. She wanted to watch every movement. Know if they found something, anything at all.

Ryan touched her arm. "Andi," he said gently, "there's nothing you can do to help. Let them do their jobs. I'll take you home."

She nodded but still couldn't tear her gaze away from the tree. She had this odd feeling that if she walked away, it would somehow all disappear.

"I'll be right back."

He left her side for the first time and went to one of the officers. He reached in his pocket and handed something over, then returned to her. "Come on," he said, urging her again with his strong but gentle voice. A few drops of rain pattered on the leaves, one touching the skin of her face, the cold drop breaking her focus. She looked over at him and nodded again.

"I'm sorry," she said. "I don't seem to know what to do with myself."

"You went into crisis mode and now you're in the

aftermath of that." He touched her arm again. "It's okay. Walk out with me and let me take you home."

"I'm in the way."

"Rain is coming. It makes their job harder. And you don't need to get soaking wet, either. You need to take care of yourself."

Andi let out a breath. She could do this. She had to get herself together. That was the only way she was going to help the situation. "All right. Let's go."

They walked through the forest, tiny drops of rain warning of a heavier deluge to come. Ryan's footsteps were strong and sure ahead of her, leading this time instead of following. The air was cold and she shivered inside her hoodie, despite the added warmth of the hunter's vest. Silently she prayed that whatever evidence had been left behind was found before the rain made it disappear.

Once they reached the service road, Ryan turned to her. "Why don't you let me drive? You're still very shaken."

"But your truck…"

"One of the guys is going to drive it back to the detachment for me." His handsome face was somber, his dark eyes showing his concern. "Andi, you're distracted. It would be safer for me to drive you. I don't want anything to happen to you."

He was right. She was distracted, and understandably so. She reached into her pocket and took out her keys. "Okay." She handed them over. "And thank you."

"Of course."

They got in her car and he started it up, then turned

the heater on. Heat came through the vents and warmed her hands and feet. She hadn't even realized that she was cold, but Ryan had known. What a blessing he was turning out to be today. Her trust had not been misplaced.

It took fifteen minutes to drive to her house, fifteen silent minutes of no conversation. She didn't know what to say to him, and she figured he didn't know what to say to her, either. It wasn't like they were close; he was Shelby's brother, but to make small talk seemed ludicrous, considering the situation. Besides, she still felt plenty fragile. When he pulled into her driveway, the awkwardness increased. She suddenly realized that by driving her home, he'd left himself without a drive back to his place, and he lived just south of Cadence Creek.

He cut the engine. "Would you like me to check out the house? Make sure everything is okay?"

The thought hadn't even occurred to her, and she was struck with fresh fear. "You mean whoever did this might…?" Concern blossomed in her chest. "Do you think they might come after me?"

"There's no reason to think that. I just want to make you feel safe and comfortable."

She looked at him closer now. His brown eyes held hers. If she had to come up with a word to describe Ryan, it would be *steady*. He never seemed to panic, kept a cool head, helped a neighbor in need and, according to Shelby, was a wonderful brother and uncle to her children. His presence today had kept her from having a full-on panic attack.

"I'm fine. I think." She tried a small smile and found it wasn't as hard as she'd imagined it would be. "You…

Gosh, Ryan. You've gone above and beyond today. You have no idea how much I appreciate it."

"You're welcome. I'd say it was my pleasure, but…" He gave a wry smile. "Well, you know what I mean."

"Nothing pleasurable about what's happened. But I do understand. Shelby always says you're on hand to help whenever she needs something. I trusted you today, and you proved me right to do so."

They sat a few moments. Then she let out a little laugh. "I suppose I need to get out of the car."

They got out. The rain that had threatened earlier was still holding off—at least, here in town. Ryan gave her the keys back. "I like this place. It's cute."

She looked around. The small deck on the back of the bungalow had been added two years ago. She'd taken a lot of pains with the garden, finally, after a few years of neglect. Joy had been hard to come by, and she'd spent a long time wondering if she deserved it. But it had returned—at least, a little of it—and she found tending the plants soothing. The house and the half acre of yard framed with maples and birches was her little oasis. She couldn't afford much, but the small improvements had made the house more "hers" than "ours" after Jim walked out on their marriage.

"Thanks," she said. "It was even prettier in the summer, when all the flowers were in bloom." Including daisies. She always made sure there were lots of daisies. Ryan looked slightly uncomfortable, and she wrinkled her brow. "What is it?"

"Do you want to call Shelby?" he asked, mirroring her frown. "So you're not alone?"

She thought about it. It was late afternoon now. Shelby would be starting dinner, waiting for her husband to come home from work, and they—Shelby, Ian and their three kids—would sit down to an evening meal.

"No, I don't think so," she replied. "She'll be making dinner. And Ian isn't home yet. She'd have to bring the kids with her..."

Ryan's face softened. "Seeing kids might be a little rough for you today."

Tears stung at his understanding. "Yes. Thank you for getting that. I love those kids, I do, but today...it's the anniversary of losing my own. It hits a little too close to home."

And yet she didn't make a move to go inside. It was as if some sort of invisible force was keeping her from walking to the front door. Maybe because if she walked in there, she'd be entirely alone, a horrible reminder of how much her life had imploded. Most days she was fine. She got up, did her job, cared for herself and, yes, found pockets of joy and contentment. That was not going to happen today, though.

She looked over at Ryan. "I hate to ask this, but... would you stay for a while? I can drive you home later."

"Of course I can."

His ready agreement was all she'd needed to put one foot in front of the other. She led him to the back step, up onto the deck and inside. They were barely in when the errant sprinkles became a steady shower, and her thoughts turned back to the crime scene. What had they found? Worse, what was being destroyed by rain?

"You can't let yourself think like that," Ryan said, somehow reading her thoughts as he toed off his boots at the front door. "You can't stop the rain."

"I know." She rolled her shoulders and let out a big breath. "I'm trying really hard to feel normal. I don't want to get caught up in my head all over again. I'm a problem solver, you know? This…inertia feels so unnatural."

"Maybe that's a good thing." He came farther into the kitchen. "I wish I could tell you there was something you could do, but you have to let the investigation take its course."

"I wish I could trust the process like you do, Ryan." She faced him and felt a little of her strength returning. "When Chelsea died, I already had so much guilt. Being questioned as if I was a bad mother really did me in. And then when no arrests were made, I lost faith. In a lot."

"I understand losing faith in the justice system when it failed you."

"In God, too," she said. "I was angry and bitter. I turned my back on Him."

"I know you stopped coming to church."

"If I'm honest, I still haven't forgiven Him. That probably sounds awful."

Since Chelsea's murder, she hadn't darkened the church door. Her elder had called and visited several times, and Shelby had tried to get her to go to services, but she'd been defiant. Even as she'd missed her church family, she'd been so angry that she couldn't bear it.

"Have you ever wanted to come back?"

She swallowed against the lump in her throat. "I'd be the biggest hypocrite in the pews. I miss the community there. And once, I thought I might be ready." It had been a strange moment for her. She'd been walking through town in the summer, forgetting it was choir practice night. The church doors were open, and the choir was singing an arrangement of "Nearer, My God, to Thee" that had reached in and touched something in her heart. "But how could I go for social reasons, knowing I was still angry with God?"

Ryan looked into her eyes, and in his she saw kindness and understanding. "Maybe because being there, in His house, might be the first step you need to take."

Maybe, but she doubted it. And she desperately wanted to change the subject. "Today's been hard," she admitted. "It's brought back so many feelings, but I can't help thinking this is a second chance to get justice for her. You're right—I've lost faith. In God. In the process. But..." She smiled. "Maybe everyone deserves a chance at redemption. Including the Cadence Creek RCMP."

He smiled back at her, and it was as if someone had turned on a light in the dim room. "I hope your faith isn't misplaced."

"Let's hope that this time the investigation has a resolution. That means I have to be strong. Just not today, you know? I don't have it in me to be strong today."

Ryan stepped forward and put a hand on her shoulder. "In my opinion, knowing you need time to be alone to let this settle *is* being strong. You're maybe the strongest woman I know."

The compliment went straight to her heart. "I try. Sometimes it's a daily struggle."

"Isn't everything?"

Then they were smiling at each other again, and Andi was glad he wasn't pushing her on the church thing. She'd asked herself many times how a loving God could do something so cruel. After a while, she'd stopped thinking about it too much. But today... Today those thoughts and feelings of betrayal had bubbled to the surface, surprising her with their sharpness.

As the moment drew out, Andi realized it was going on six o'clock. Where had the hours gone? She rubbed her hands together; they were no longer icy cold. "Well, being strong means taking care of myself, which means making sure I eat. Why don't I cook us both some dinner?"

"I don't want to be a bother."

"After today? I owe you more than a meal." She felt like being honest yet again. "Besides, other than the company, sometimes it's hard to muster up the motivation to cook for one. Really, Ryan, I'd like to." She smiled shyly. "I think I'm a passable cook. I won't poison you."

He chuckled a bit. "Then I won't say no."

She started pulling out ingredients to make a simple meal of pork chops and mushroom gravy, mashed potatoes and vegetables. Ryan insisted on helping by peeling the carrots, and before long, everything was bubbling on the stove. Some of the tension of the day melted away in the busyness of it all; they sat down to eat, and Ryan said a quick grace before digging in. Andi was surprised she was able to eat, but Ryan's company was so calming that, after the first few hesitant bites, she found herself quite hungry and went on to finish the meal. When they were done, Ryan even insisted on helping clean up, drying the dishes after she washed them.

He'd made what might have been an awful few hours of being alone tolerable. More than tolerable. Enjoyable. Which, considering the circumstances, felt like a miracle.

It was dark when she finally drove him home, locking her door and leaving the outside light on for her return. But once she left him at his house, the car seemed strangely empty and the hole in her chest from earlier in the afternoon opened again. Without the distraction of Ryan, the events of the day were front and center in her mind. The shock and fear were not as intense as earlier, but she couldn't escape what had happened or what it might mean. She was going to have to relive the case all over again, but if it meant finding Chelsea's murderer, then she would do it. She had to. She'd been through the worst thing she could imagine and survived. She'd survive this, too.

And yet when she parked her car and got out, a strange sensation skittered over her body, sending a chill down her spine.

She couldn't escape the feeling that someone had been here in her absence. And that, somehow, the toy in the woods was less about Chelsea and more about her. But who would want to hurt her in this way? And why?

Chapter Three

Ryan couldn't stop thinking about Andi.

In the days that followed, he kept his distance. For one, he was a cop and her daughter's murder case had been reopened. For another, he'd enjoyed the dinner with her more than was advisable. There were a million reasons not to let things get too familiar. Potential conflict of interest, the fact that she was his sister's best friend and, most of all, the fact that she intimidated him. Not because she was an intimidating person, but because she'd been through so much. He wasn't sure he was ready to date someone with that much baggage, and if he were being honest, sitting down to dinner with her had felt far too domestic and couple-like. She'd taken his hand before he'd said grace, and it had shaken him. Made him think about things he had no business thinking. Not about his sister's best friend. Not about someone who was part of an open investigation, either.

In the weeks following Chelsea's death, he'd seen the way grief had overwhelmed her. Shelby had cried on his shoulder more than once, worried about her friend. Today he'd seen that same look of pain on Andi's face. He had his own feelings about Chelsea's case that still weighed heavily. He'd had nightmares for weeks. He wasn't sure he could handle her emotions, as well.

So he spent the next few days at the detachment, keeping his eyes peeled for news of the investigation. So far not much had turned up. A few footprints that could easily have belonged to hunters in the area. No eyewitnesses to anything. And the DNA tests on the stuffed animal weren't back yet, though it was doubtful they would show anything. The rain hadn't held off for long, either. It was possible some evidence had been destroyed by the weather. Now they'd never know.

He sat in the church pew with his family, listening to the sermon with one ear and singing along with the hymns, but he felt an unusual restlessness. The Sunday service was generally a source of comfort and community, a place to come together in hope and celebration. Today his thoughts wouldn't settle. There was something about Andi's case that wasn't sitting right, but he couldn't put his finger on it, and nothing in the evidence was nudging him in a particular direction. He didn't discount intuition, of course, but he needed more than that. He figured that he'd go over the old file again and see if anything stood out.

The biggest surprise, however, was that Andi was here, sitting in the back. He hadn't known until his family had stood to take the collection and he'd spied her in the corner. Had she considered what he'd said about showing up first and going from there? He understood

her anger and questioning. She'd been through something horrific. If being in His house could help, he was
glad she'd come inside.

After church was over, and Shelby's kids came back
upstairs from Sunday school, the family made their way
to the door. He saw Andi standing alone, and his heart
gave a little thump. It wasn't right that she didn't have
family here with her. He knew from Shelby that she
was an only child and her parents lived in Calgary. It
wasn't that far away—ninety minutes, maybe—but it
did mean that on a day-to-day basis she didn't have the
kind of support she might need. He didn't know what
he'd do without his family. That she'd suffered without
her church family, too, made his heart hurt.

"Uncle Ryan, give me a piggyback," demanded Carson, who was six.

"Uncle Ryan, give me a piggyback, please," reminded
Shelby, who turned around and grinned at her brother.
Her smile faltered. "You look like something's bother-
ing you. What's up?"

Was he that transparent? "I'm fine. Just thinking.
Did you know Andi was coming today?" He squatted
down when Carson echoed "please" and hefted the boy
onto his back.

"No, but I'm glad she did. She's refused for so long.
I wonder what changed?" At the door, they both shook
hands with the minister before going outside into the
late-September sunshine, and Ryan was spared from
answering.

He dropped Carson off once they were in the parking lot and then went to Andi, who was walking to her

car. There was something off about her. She looked small somehow.

"Andi. Hey, Andi!"

She turned around, and a smile bloomed on her face as he approached. "Oh, hi," she answered.

"I'm surprised to see you. But pleased."

She blushed a little. "Don't get too excited. I was thinking about what you said the other night."

"And how was it?"

Her gaze slid away from his. "Weird."

Heat touched his cheeks; he hadn't meant to press and now she was uncomfortable. "Anyway, how're you doing?"

She shrugged, looking back at him with dull eyes. "I'm okay, I guess. Waiting for news. And…reliving things. That's been hard."

He appreciated that she was honest and not insisting everything was fine. He'd been experiencing some of the same, though from a wholly different perspective. As a new officer, being on the original scene had left an indelible mark on his soul. Going out there again, knowing there was new evidence… He'd started going over the initial investigation, both the file and in his head. Wondering if they'd missed something. And reliving some of the shock and grief. He supposed any murder would be hard, but that of a child was worse.

"Of course it's been rough."

"And…" She hesitated, then shrugged. "Never mind. It's silly."

"If there's something bothering you, I promise it's not silly," he urged.

She bit down on her lip, looked at the ground and then up again. "I know it's probably stress. I just… I get the feeling that someone is watching me all the time."

Ryan's alert level went up a notch. "Have you noticed anything unusual? Around your house or at work or anything?"

She shook her head. "That's just it. Everything has been perfect. Almost too perfect. It's just a feeling, and I know as well as you do that feelings have nothing to do with proof."

She was right. "Maybe not, but I never discount gut feelings. Maybe it *is* stress from reopening the case. Or feeling unsafe because of the rabbit. Still, you should be careful and aware of your surroundings, okay?"

She nodded. "Thank you for believing me."

He nodded. "Why wouldn't I?"

At that moment Shelby came over, Carson scuffing his shoes in the gravel and her one-year-old baby, Gillian, in her arms while three-year-old Macy held her hand. "Hey, Andi, we're all going to the Wagon Wheel for lunch. Do you want to join us?"

Andi started to shake her head, but Ryan cleared his throat. "Why don't you? It's like you're part of the family anyway." Something he'd do well to remember. Family. Friend.

Shelby nodded. "I've missed seeing you around, and so have the kids. Mom and Dad are going, too. A nice big family lunch where none of us have to cook or clean up."

When Andi finally nodded, a knot of tension released in Ryan's chest. Andi didn't look okay, and while her feelings might be related to past trauma, he didn't want to assume so. He believed her when she said she felt watched. Today, he'd keep his eyes open. She'd already lost so much. She didn't deserve to lose her sense of safety again.

It was dark when Andi finally made her way home. Lunch at the Wagon Wheel had gone on until nearly two o'clock, and then Shelby and Ian had invited her back to their place to spend the afternoon. It was a beautiful, warm fall day, and they sat on the back deck with glasses of lemonade while Carson and Macy played with a friend in the backyard and baby Gillian slept in a nearby playpen, exhausted from the action and the fresh air. Around four, Ryan left to get ready for his night shift, and to her surprise, she'd felt his absence. At lunch and during the afternoon he'd been a steady part of the conversation, always adding a smile and a laugh and paying attention to the kids when they wanted their "Uncle Ry."

Afternoon turned into dinner—Shelby had put a pot roast in her Crock-Pot before church—and before Andi knew it, her belly was full, dark was falling, and she had to start thinking about getting home. Tomorrow was another workday. Still, for several hours today she had managed to almost forget everything that was happening. The Davenport family had always been good to her and for her in that way.

She finished drying a plate and reached up into the cupboard to put it away when Shelby faced her, wiping her hands on a dish towel.

"Something's going on with you. You've been super quiet. Are you okay?" Her pretty face was puckered with concern. "Is it this time of year? I know it's hard." She put her hand on Andi's. "Were the kids too much?"

Andi didn't want all of Cadence Creek to know what was going on, but Shelby was her best friend and the closest thing to a sister she'd ever had. Not telling her seemed odd. She closed the cupboard door and let out a sigh. "It's not you. They've reopened the case," she said quietly, looking over her shoulder. This wasn't something she wanted to talk about with the little ones around.

"But that's wonderful news! Is there new evidence? What's happened?"

Andi knew it was great news, but it was hard to be excited when grief constantly revisited her, dragging her down into the darkness. "Someone left Chelsea's bunny at the scene," she said. "Very deliberately. They're testing it now for DNA and they processed the scene, but so far it's just waiting. Investigations never go as fast as they do on TV."

Shelby patted her arm. "Right? If only this could be like an hour of *Law and Order* and everything tied up with a confession at the end. But still, after so much time… This is good, right?"

"I know." She smiled a little. "I'm just finding it difficult. I mean, this time of year is always tough, but this adds a whole other element. This wasn't an accidental find. Whoever put it there meant for me to find it. I'm sure of that."

"Do you think you're in danger?" Shelby's voice was heavy with concern.

Andi shook her head. "I'm sure I'm not. Why would I be?" But the other alternative was that perhaps someone was playing mind games with her. She didn't like that thought one bit.

"Has there been anything else?" Shelby frowned. "I mean, why leave it now, unless..." She tapped her lip. "Whoever did it must know you go out there every year."

Andi sighed. "That's no secret. I think the whole town knows. It's hard to keep anything private in a town this small."

"Which makes this whole thing all the more confusing."

"You're telling me."

"But you're okay?"

Andi nodded. "I called Ryan when it happened. He reported it, and he's been great. You were right, Shel. He's a great brother and friend."

Shelby looked at her closely. "Any hope for anything more?"

Andi thought back to the way his deep brown eyes had held hers that night at her house and how they'd laughed over dinner. It had been pleasant, more than pleasant, and anyone could see he was an attractive guy.

"I don't think so. I'm not ready, for starters."

"Not ready? Girl, you're thirty-five and you've been divorced for six years. You could do worse than my brother."

She smiled at that. "I know. It's nothing against

Ryan. I'm just carrying a lot of baggage. About Chelsea, and about Jim, too. The thought of going through that again…"

Shelby took pity on Andi's distress and took a step forward to give her a small hug. "I know the divorce did a number on you. Forget I said anything. Are you going to be okay?"

"Of course I am." A warmth spread through her at her friend's love and support. "Being here today was just what the doctor ordered."

Shelby and her family lived southwest of Cadence Creek and about five minutes away from Ryan. Their acreage included a small pasture where their two horses grazed and a creek that flowed along the perimeter. Andi was feeling more relaxed than usual when she began the drive north toward town. The company and talking to Shelby about the situation had helped so much. So had the fresh air and wonderful meal. She had the radio on low and tapped her fingers along with the beat as she passed the church. She'd only met two cars on the road, so it was a surprise when headlights appeared in her rearview mirror.

That was all it took for the nagging feeling to return, settling low in her stomach, and she tightened her fingers on the wheel. "Relax, Andi," she murmured to herself. "It's just another car. Stop being so hypervigilant."

But the other vehicle was catching up. Where had it come from, anyway? She bit down on her lip. It was coming on fast…too fast. Her pulse raced as she considered her options. The shoulder was not wide enough for her to pull over. She knew she couldn't stop. The only thing she could really do was keep a steady speed and hope whoever it was pulled by to pass—and that there wouldn't be any oncoming cars when that happened.

The car had its high beams on, and they glared in her mirror. She reached up and flipped the lever on the rearview mirror to dull the light, but it didn't stop the alarm at how close the car was now. She couldn't panic, but she was close to freaking out and tried to remain steady. If they got any closer, they'd be in her trunk!

The car jolted as the vehicle behind her nudged her bumper, and instinctively she tapped the brakes and tried to correct with the wheel. Her tires touched the gravel shoulder, and the panic she'd been holding back threatened to break free as her wheels grabbed and spun in the dirt. She'd just gained control when the car came on again, once more tapping her bumper, and Andi started to cry. Cold fear raced through her veins. Who was trying to hurt her? Were they going to run her off the road? She said a quick prayer. "What do I do, God? Please, help me."

The lights came on again, but at the last minute the car pulled to the left and flew past her, so fast that she couldn't make out a plate or even the model. In seconds even the taillights were gone, and it was almost as if she'd imagined the whole thing.

She kept going, speed steady, until she reached Diamondback Ranch. The porch lights offered a tiny beacon of security and safety, and the top of the wide drive provided enough space for her to pull over. It wasn't until she put the car in Park that the shakes started. It took a full five minutes for her to stop trembling enough to pull out her phone.

She called 911. "Hello? This is Andi Wallace. Someone tried to run me off the road."

As she gave the details of her location, she realized something vital. She hadn't been wrong the other day. This wasn't about Chelsea. This was about her.

For whatever reason, she was now the target.

Ryan was on duty when the call came through his radio. Since he was closest to her location, he pulled a U-turn and headed toward Diamondback Ranch. The unsettled feeling of earlier came roaring back. He kept wondering about that bunny nailed to the tree. While he didn't like to operate on assumption, it was certainly clear to him that the only person who would do such a thing was the murderer. It had been put there on or shortly before the anniversary of Chelsea's death. Now Andi was being followed and threatened. What had changed to make him—or her—come out of the woodwork? Why, and even more specific, why now? He wished the DNA results would come back and they might find something. So far the scene had created nothing but dead ends. He'd always subscribed to the principle that the perpetrator left some sort of clue at the scene and took something away with them, too. But when the scene was in the middle of the woods, at an undetermined time, with no witnesses... Evidence could disappear. Nature was like that.

He turned on his lights but not his siren as he approached the ranch, so that Andi would know it was help arriving and not more trouble. After radioing in, he got out of the car and went to her window. The look of stark relief on her face when she rolled down the window and saw it was him was one he'd never forget. She was terrified.

"You all right?" he asked, knowing it was a foolish question because clearly she was not. "Are you hurt?"

She shook her head. "No. Not that way. I stayed on the road. I'm just…shaken."

There was a wobble in her voice that went straight to his heart and brought out all his protective instincts. He wished he could help her out of the car and hold her in his arms until she stopped shaking, but that wouldn't be right. Not professionally. And she was Shelby's friend. She'd asked him for help as a friend, because she trusted him. No way would he break that trust.

"Sit tight for a few minutes, okay?"

He shone his light around the car. The only damage he could see was on her bumper. There was a slight dent, and a little bit of paint was rubbed there. Black. He went to her window again. "What color was the car? Do you remember?"

"Black, I think. I was so worried about staying on the road that the only thing that is crystal clear is how bright the headlights were." She sniffled. "Sorry. I don't mean to cry."

"It's a natural way to release some of the adrenaline," he answered, keeping his voice gentle. "You're okay, Andi. There's no big damage to your car, just a little paint on your bumper."

But they both knew the damage to the car wasn't the

terrible thing about all of this. It was the fact that someone had deliberately targeted her, tried to frighten her, do her harm. What if she hadn't been able to keep the car on the road? He didn't like to think of what might have happened to her.

"Are you able to drive to your house?" he asked. "I can follow you. Take a statement."

She nodded. "Yes. I can manage."

"Okay. I'll be right behind you and I'll see you there, okay?"

He got back in his cruiser and stayed on her tail as they made their way to her home. The entire drive he kept thinking about possibilities. Perhaps this was random. There was nothing proving that tonight was linked to the reopened investigation. But Ryan also wasn't a big believer in coincidences. Which meant the alternative was that whoever had been driving that car had known where she was, had known when she left, and made sure they scared the life out of her. They'd been following her, and then they'd deliberately put her in jeopardy.

Once at her house, she parked the car, shut off the lights and got out. He followed suit and went to her. "Okay?" he asked.

"Fine. Well, not fine. Trying to be more angry than afraid. That's easier."

"Let's go inside. I'll take your statement where it's more comfortable."

She led the way, pulling out her key and unlocking the door in the dark. She hadn't left the porch light on; he supposed she hadn't expected to be gone so long when she left for church this morning. She was still in her church clothes, a gray dress that looked like a long sweater with a belt at the waist, and black tights that disappeared into low-heeled black boots. As he stepped inside in all his gear, she paused and unzipped the boots, putting them on a mat and stepping forward in her bare feet.

He swallowed tightly. He hated that she was going through this again and admired her strength.

"Do you want coffee or tea or something?" she asked.

"No, thanks. I wish I could stay, but I'm on duty. Once I take your statement, I'll have to go."

She nodded. "I know. Sorry."

"Are you afraid to stay alone?"

She lifted her chin. "Yes, but I'm not going to let someone chase me out of my own house. I'm just not going to sleep much tonight, that's all."

"I'll try to drive by a few times, if that helps."

She smiled a little and her face relaxed. "It does. It's comforting to know that you're watching out for me. Shelby always says what a good brother you are."

He grinned. "Oh, I'm not so sure about that."

They moved into the kitchen and sat at the table so Ryan could take down all the information he needed. Sadly, there wasn't much. She relayed everything that had happened, but it had been dark, and it had happened quickly. Of course, there was always the possibility that the other car had sustained some damage, so he'd make sure to contact any local body shops to see if anyone brought a black car in for repair. A few minutes later, the statement was done. Ryan had never felt so ineffective.

"If you think of anything else, please let us know," he said, getting up from the table. "And like I said, I'll drive by a few times tonight to check on things."

"Thank you, Ryan. For everything."

"I wish it were more. I wish I had all the answers for you," he admitted. Their gazes locked and he felt that pull again. He stepped away, clearing his throat. "Lock up after me."

"I will."

She showed him to the door, and he left without turning back again. There was something about Andi that made him want to be able to fix everything. Fixing was what he did. His job was to make things right, protect people from harm. All people. But he was quickly starting to realize that Andi wasn't just anyone. She was special. And she couldn't be. Not if he were to do his job objectively and impartially.

He got into his cruiser and headed out to finish his shift.

Chapter Four

Two days later the DNA report came in on the stuffed rabbit. Sergeant Ben Rogers was the lead on the case, and he pulled Ryan into his office when the news came.

"We knew DNA would be a long shot," Rogers said, a frown marring his forehead. "That being said, we did have two positive matches. One being Chelsea's and the other her father's. Nothing unexpected."

Ryan sat back in his chair, disappointed. "Whoever did this was very careful. For touch DNA to last that long, that stuffed toy had to be kept in pristine condition."

"Like a trophy," Rogers agreed, and the implications of that settled around them. "Still, I think we should pay a visit to Jim Wallace and update him on the case. Do you know if Andi has been in touch with him at all since the nineteenth?"

Ryan hadn't thought to ask. "I don't think so, but I can't be sure." He hesitated, then voiced what was on his mind. "You know we looked at him during the initial investigation."

"Yeah. The evidence didn't add up to anything, though. I'll admit there was something off about him, but when people are under a lot of stress, that's understandable. I'd like to inform him of the latest developments and let him know we've reopened the case."

"Of course." Ryan bit his tongue. He wasn't sure what kind of man could walk out on a grieving wife and mother, and he didn't have a lot of respect for the guy. However, Jim had also lost his daughter. He deserved to know that the case had been reopened. "You know, one of the things missing from the start was any sense of motive. Who would want to do this to a little girl? Who would want to hurt Jim and Andi this badly?" He pursed his lips. "And who would hang on to a token like this for seven years, then suddenly choose to reveal it…to Andi?" He looked Sergeant Rogers in the eyes. "Whoever it was knew that Andi visited there each year on the anniversary. They knew she was driving home the other night. Yeah, we need to talk to Jim, but everything in my gut tells me this has to do with Andi, not him. And I can't imagine why."

Ben tapped his pen on his desk. "She went through some tough questioning at the time. She'd made mistakes, no doubt about it. When the search focused around Chelsea wandering away, that was one thing. Once her body was found, though…" Rogers's gaze held Ryan's. "You don't forget a day like that."

"No, sir," Ryan murmured, "you don't." Andi had been beside herself with grief. Her parents had been with her since Chelsea had gone missing. Seeing the tight knot of her family huddled together in their shared distress had done something to him. Something he could never get back. Not everything broken could be fixed.

Rogers ran a hand through his gray hair and got up from behind his desk. "All right, then. Let's go pay Mr. Wallace a visit and update him on what's happening."

Ryan rose as well and rolled his shoulders. Fine with him. And while he was there, he was going to see if Jim Wallace drove a black car with any damage on the front bumper. It was just a hunch, but it was worth checking out. Someone was trying to scare Andi, possibly even hurt her. A troubled ex was as good a place to start as any. If nothing else, he could rule him out.

Jim Wallace lived in a tiny bungalow about two minutes off Highway 22, north of Cadence Creek and closer to his work in Red Deer as a farm equipment salesman. Ryan and Ben caught him just after he arrived home for the day. As they approached the door, Jim stepped out onto the landing. It was sagging a bit and in need of a fresh paint job. The whole place looked a bit run-down in comparison to Andi's small but well-tended home. "Can I help you?" Jim asked.

Ryan studied the man, so close in age to himself. Sandy brown hair, around five-ten, medium build. He looked pleasant enough, he supposed. When Chelsea had disappeared, Ryan had noticed that the man had been agitated and jumpy, but considering the circumstances, it wasn't an unusual reaction. Jim had said repeatedly that he wanted to be out searching, doing something, but the RCMP and SAR had tried to keep civilians out of the way.

Ryan had a strange sense of empathy toward Jim, he realized. The guy had lost his daughter and, a year later, his wife. Had to be tough on any man. He could respect that and still not like him for walking away.

"Jim Wallace?"

"Sergeant Rogers, you know it's me."

Ben smiled. "Yes, sir. You have a minute, Jim?"

"Sure. You might as well come in."

Ryan followed Jim and Ben inside, and then Ben made introductions. "Jim, you remember Corporal Davenport, don't you?"

"Shelby's brother."

Ryan gave a nod. Ben would do the talking. Ryan would step back, observe.

They took a seat in the living room, on a sofa that had seen better days. Jim wasn't much of a housekeeper, Ryan noticed. There was a pile of unfolded clothes on a chair, some dirty dishes on a TV tray. It looked as if the floor hadn't been vacuumed in several days. But Jim, he noticed, was neat and tidy. Pressed khakis, button-down shirt, trimmed hair, no scruff.

"Jim, there's been a development in your daughter's case."

Jim's face tensed. "After so long?"

"On September 19, your ex-wife discovered one of Chelsea's stuffed toys at the crime scene. Did you know she went there each year on the anniversary of Chelsea's death?"

Jim shook his head, and his lip trembled. "No. It doesn't surprise me, though. Andi was so devoted to her."

"We ran DNA tests on the toy. It came up positive for yours and Chelsea's."

Jim's eyebrows pulled together in confusion. "Mine and hers? After all this time? I don't understand."

"It's unusual for DNA to stay on an object for so long," Ben agreed. "We were hoping to find someone else's. Whoever had the toy was very careful to keep their own DNA off of it."

Jim's lip wobbled even more as he took a deep breath. "I don't understand. It's bad enough they killed my daughter. Why torture us like this now?" He put his hands over his face for a moment, then let out a breath and looked at Ben again. "How is Andi handling this? She must be a wreck."

"It's been a difficult week," Ben replied. "Have you spoken to Andi at all lately?"

Jim shook his head. "Naw. Things didn't end well with us. I haven't spoken to her in ages. I don't remember when."

"You living here alone, Jim?" Ryan asked. He'd noticed one of those plug-in air fresheners in the corner, a lavender scent. There were curtains in the kitchen, too, ones with little flowers on them. Nothing major, but Jim didn't seem the type for floral patterns and scents.

"Just me, myself and I," he said lightly, but something flashed on his face that made Ryan pay attention. Something told him that Jim might live alone, but he wasn't a fan of the situation.

"We'll keep you updated, of course, on any developments in the case," Ben said. "I'm sorry we've had to trouble you after all this time."

"If it means finding who murdered my daughter, it's worth it," Jim answered.

They got up to leave. Ben gave Jim his card and told him to call if he thought of anything at all. Ryan led the way outside, hesitating at the bottom of the porch steps.

Jim drove a black older-model sedan. As Ben finished talking to Jim, Ryan did a walk-around of the vehicle, stopping to look at the front bumper. No cracks, dents or silver paint from Andi's car. The local body shops hadn't repaired a car of that description, either. Looked like that particular incident was at a dead end, too. Ryan clenched his teeth. They were missing something. Something important. Why couldn't they see it?

The nurses at the Cadence Creek Medical Clinic took turns working Thursday and Friday evenings during the week. Thursday was Andi's night to stay late, since they stayed open until eight for walk-ins. By the time the last patient had been seen, it was twenty past; Andi and the other staff then went through the closing rituals in preparation for the next day's appointments. As a result, it was quarter to nine by the time everyone exited the building and went to their cars. Andi glanced over her shoulder before she unlocked the door, then peered into the back seat once the dome light came on. Ever since Sunday night, she'd been on high alert, checking her surroundings, constantly watching the rearview mirror. Add that into the not sleeping, and she was definitely on edge.

The drive from the clinic to her house was a short one; sometimes in the summer she walked if the weather wasn't too hot. She didn't on her long days, though. The payoff of working nine to eight thirty on Thursdays was that she had Friday afternoons off. Tomorrow she'd work until one and then be off for the weekend. Not that her weekends were exciting, but still. Tomorrow afternoon she planned to enjoy the forecast warm weather on her deck with a pumpkin-spiced coffee and a book. Something to relax her after the stress of the week.

Her headlights flashed over the yard as she pulled in the driveway. Generally, her parking spot was right in front of the garage. Once snow came, she'd park inside, but for now her lawn mower and other yard equipment took up space in the single-car garage. Tonight, as her headlights hit the garage door, she was greeted with black spray paint.

PEEKABOO I SEE YOU was sprayed in all caps, and then followed by several curse words and offensive names.

Andi had felt afraid most of the time since the rabbit was found. The words only highlighted the sense of being followed that had plagued her for the last several days. As she stared at the epithets shouting at her from her door, her breath caught, and the letters swam in front of her eyes as she shoved the car in Park.

All the muscles in her legs tightened as she fought for air, the panic attack hitting with a brutality that would have cut her off at the knees had she been standing. She didn't know how long she sat there, the car running, trying to breathe as horrible scenarios flashed through her brain. Finally, sometime later, her breath began to slow and she gulped it in, punctuated by sobs.

For a few weeks now she'd been as strong as she could be, but tonight she was not okay.

Andi waited another few minutes and forced herself to pay attention to each part of her body, mentally relaxing her muscles. As the shock and panic eased, another emotion took their place. Anger. Anger at whoever thought she needed to be intimidated and tortured, as if losing her child wasn't enough. Anger, too, at life and at God. It didn't seem fair that this should be happening to her all over again. How much was one person supposed to take?

Then she let out a breath. "It's okay to be angry. It's okay to be scared. Get a grip, Andi. You're stronger than this."

She said it out loud and then frowned. Was she? She was living life over her shoulder right now, afraid for herself, reliving her grief and going through it alone. As she sat in the car with her lights illuminating the hateful message, she'd never felt more forsaken.

She got out of the car and left the lights on, then slammed the door. At least this might be another clue. The DNA results had yielded absolutely nothing. She picked up her cell phone in shaky hands and sent Ryan a text outlining the situation and assuring him she was fine, even though she felt anything but. She took a picture of the door in the light of her headlights and sent that, too. There was no sense in calling the cop shop; there was nothing they could do about it tonight. She had nothing to clean off the disgusting words, anyway.

Tomorrow after work, she'd stop at the hardware store and get some materials. If the paint wouldn't come off, she'd repaint the thing. It needed it anyway.

She refused to be beaten. Tonight she'd fallen down. Given in to the fear. That was over now.

A ding announced a new message, and a quick glance showed Ryan had replied.

Don't touch anything. I'll be by in the morning.

She moved her thumbs rapidly to type a reply.

I have to work at nine.

Her phone rang. "Hi," she said, hoping her voice didn't tremble.

"Are you home?"

"I'm still at my car."

"I don't like you going home after dark," he said.

A little flutter of warmth went through her body, but she pushed it away. "I appreciate the concern, but I work late on Thursdays. Believe me, I'm being careful."

There was quiet. Then, "Are you sleeping?"

"Some." There was no point in lying about it.

"Listen, we can come over tomorrow morning and check this out. As long as you're okay with us doing that while you're at work."

She thought back to a few days earlier when Ryan had come by with Ben Rogers to fill her in on the DNA results. At least the cops were taking this very seriously. Plus, she trusted Ryan. "I'm okay with that."

"Don't disturb anything. Walk right from your car to your door and follow the same path tomorrow when you come out."

"Okay." She paused. "Ryan?"

"Yes?"

"Will you stay on the phone with me until I get inside?" She hated asking, but having him on the line made her feel less alone.

"Of course."

She hit the key fob to lock the car. With the phone still pressed to her ear, she walked straight to the steps and up to the back door. The porch light was on this time—she had turned it on before leaving this morning, knowing she would be late. Once she stepped inside, she flipped on a light switch and then shut the door, locking the dead bolt behind her.

She hated living this way, in constant fear. She was a strong woman, but this was wearing her down. Anger could only carry her forward for so long.

"I'm inside," she whispered. "Thank you, Ryan."

"We'll be there bright and early," he replied. "Don't worry."

Andi woke from broken sleep just after six, feeling utterly unrested and anxious. More police today, this time because her garage door had been tagged. This was the kind of thing that would normally rate a single cop and an incident report, with the assumption of some kids making mischief. But because of Chelsea and the things that had been happening lately, this was suddenly a big deal. Not to mention the message itself.

I see you definitely supported her feeling of being followed. She was going to have to be even more aware.
Look for anything out of the ordinary.

At least at work she had a break from all of it and got
to deal with other people's troubles. She dragged herself out of bed and hit the shower, and then she made a
pot of coffee. The scent of it perked her up a little bit,
and by the time she'd made her oatmeal, the brew was
ready, and she poured her first revivifying cup.

She had that one and another, then a glass of water
to take her vitamins. She swallowed them and put the
bottles back in the cupboard. Other than a single, small
bottle of ibuprofen, there were no other drugs in her
cabinet. Her throat tightened. A simple cold pill had
knocked her out the morning Chelsea had disappeared.
After that day she couldn't bear to have any medication on the premises. If she could go back, she'd leave
the medication alone, make herself another cup of tea
with lemon and honey, and stay awake. If she hadn't
fallen asleep, Chelsea might still be here. She'd never
forgiven herself for that. How could she?

The third cup of coffee went in her travel mug, and
then she had to get ready for work. By the time she came
out of the bedroom in her scrubs, there were two cruis-
ers in her yard. She took a calming breath. Was it wrong
to be thinking about the neighbors at this moment and
wondering if they were all speculating wildly about
what was happening? Other than Shelby and Ryan, she
hadn't spoken to anyone about finding the stuffed rabbit. So far, the media hadn't caught wind of any developments in the case. But Andi knew it was only a matter

of time before it became news. She dreaded facing public scrutiny all over again.

She stepped outside and four heads instantly looked up at the sound of the door opening. "Good morning," she offered, trying to act as if this was as normal as apple pie.

"Good morning, Mrs. Wallace." The sergeant from the other day gave her a nod.

"Sergeant Rogers."

She went to her car, a straight line and away from the garage, just as Ryan had suggested. Ryan smiled at her. "Wow. Interesting use of language, wouldn't you agree?"

There were words scrawled on her garage door that would never cross her lips. "Inventive, certainly," she replied and lifted her chin. "Someone doesn't like me very much, Corporal." She looked at the door and then back at him again. "And they're trying to intimidate me."

"It looks that way, yes."

The *peekaboo* words were an additional sting. "I know it's probably no different than any other child, but we used to play peekaboo with Chelsea when she was a baby. She'd laugh, you know, those big baby belly laughs." Her heart ached, remembering. "The choice of words seems very deliberate."

"We're going to talk to your neighbors. See if anyone noticed anything yesterday. It certainly seems as if whoever did this knew you wouldn't be at home. Maybe someone saw a strange car on the street."

"It's a small town. I've worked late on Thursdays

at the clinic for ten years. My schedule is really predictable. Pretty much anyone would know I wasn't at home."

Ryan nodded. "We shouldn't be very long. I know you want to be able to clean this off."

"I'm done at one. I figured I'd run into the hardware store for supplies after work."

He left the other officers alone and went to stand with her by her car. "Do you want some help? I'm off at three. I could give you a hand." He turned and looked at the door and then back at her. "It's going to take some elbow grease."

She knew she should say no. She was starting to rely on Ryan's help too much. And yet the idea of coming home to scrub off the paint all alone left a hollow feeling in her chest. Truth was, she felt alone much of the time. Normally she was able to hide it, but recently, with everything happening, she'd noticed the emptiness more than usual. "I'd like that, I think. In the meantime, though, I have to go to work."

"Drive safely," he said, stepping back.

She opened the door and put her purse on the passenger seat, then slid inside and set her coffee in the cup holder. Ryan stepped forward and shut her door for her, and when she started the engine and began to back out of her driveway, he waved.

Yep. Relying on him too much, but shaky enough to not care. She needed someone, and right now Ryan Davenport felt like a gift from God. She'd be foolish to turn her back on that kind of support and friendship.

Chapter Five

By the time Andi returned home from work, it was two o'clock. She'd stopped at the hardware store in Cadence Creek and bought a few different materials. Then she'd popped into the bakery and picked up two thick ham sandwiches and a box of cappuccino cupcakes from Avery Shepard. Avery's baked goods were the best and a real treat. After the last week, Andi figured she deserved something special, particularly since her planned afternoon of a book and yummy coffee had gone out the window. Besides, if Ryan was going to help her get the paint off her garage door, the least she could do was give him a sandwich and a cupcake as payment.

She stowed the sandwiches in the fridge and went to change out of her scrubs into a pair of old jeans and a soft fleece that had seen better days and was now used for "dirty" chores. There was a burn hole in one sleeve where a spark from a neighborhood bonfire had landed, and a stain down the side from when she'd repainted the shutters. The memories took her back to brighter days, when she and Jim had participated in neighborhood events. Time was divided into two sections for her now: before Chelsea's death and after. The old fleece was from the before time, and she just didn't have the heart to throw it away. The solvents she'd picked up to get rid of the graffiti were strong. She wasn't about to wear good clothing, even if it meant looking a little worse for wear in front of Ryan. She wasn't trying to impress him, after all.

She stared at her face in the mirror. She looked tired, and she gave her lips a swipe of gloss and wondered if she should reapply her mascara. Her heart gave a little thump at the thought of him coming by again. But she shouldn't be thinking that way. He was Shelby's brother, and he was just being neighborly. Offering a helping hand, as he often did within the community. It would be foolish to read more into it than that. She was just being needy.

At three fifteen, his pickup rolled into the yard. He'd changed, too, into jeans and a hooded sweatshirt. Goodness, he was attractive. His dark eyes and easy smile perked her up more readily than the fresh coffee she'd brewed thirty minutes ago.

"Hungry?" she asked. "I got some food in town. We can have something to eat before we start, if you want."

He shrugged. "I grabbed something on my lunch break. I'm good, if you want to do this first while we still have lots of daylight."

She was hungry, but she could hold off another couple of hours. "I'll get the stuff I bought. The guy at the hardware store said to try gentle stuff first, and if it's stubborn, head for the paint thinner." She grinned. The man behind the counter had been pleasant and funny, making the awful task a little less horrible. She was ready to roll up her sleeves and get to work.

Andi got out the materials and tried to ignore the hateful words marring the garage door. The incident on the road had shaken her safety, but this felt so personal. F-bombs in black spray paint and names that no woman should ever be called were scrawled over the surface, not to mention the insinuation that she was being watched. She held a rag in her hand and looked over at Ryan. "Why would anyone do this to me? I don't know who I could have hurt so badly that this is how they feel about me." She sighed. "I'm nowhere near perfect, but I try to be a good person. Kind and compassionate. I don't understand this kind of hate being in someone's heart."

Ryan nodded. "Generally, I find people lash out like this for one of two reasons. They're either angry or hurt or…"

He didn't finish the sentence.

"Or what?"

He met her gaze. "Or they're just bad people. I try to put myself in others' shoes, but sometimes I have to admit that there are bad people who do bad things, and it's not up to me to find redemption for them. There are psychopaths and sociopaths and people with no respect for human life."

She stared at him for a long time, realizing suddenly how his faith in humanity had to suffer, being in his line of work. "So you've had your faith tested, too," she murmured. She'd taken Ryan's advice to heart and had gone to church, but that trip had been rewarded by someone trying to run her off the road. She just didn't understand how this could be the work of a loving God. The old platitudes ran through her head, contradicting her. Honestly, she was just so confused. The only thing holding her together was putting one foot in front of the other, hour by hour.

Ryan smiled at her. "Occasionally, I suppose," he answered. "The good news is there are a lot more people who just need help and understanding, so I find my job quite fulfilling."

They started cleaning with a gentle spray cleaner, using rags and rubbing in circular motions, trying to remove the paint. It was soon clear that the spray solution wasn't up to the task. The black paint clung stubbornly to the white door. "Acetone?" she asked, her heart sinking a bit.

"I think so. You might end up with damage to the white paint as well, but it's nothing that a fresh coat won't fix."

They went to work, going slowly and carefully to remove the black and preserve the coat beneath. The day was beautiful; not too warm, with that lovely crisp fall feeling in the air and a bright blue sky above that mellowed as the afternoon drew out and the dinner hour approached. The chemical seemed to work well against the stubborn paint, and Andi felt her arm relaxing into the motion of rubbing in little circles as they made progress.

"Sergeant Rogers and I went to see your ex the other day," Ryan said casually.

Andi looked over. He was still rubbing in a steady rhythm, completely relaxed. "I see."

"We thought we should update him on the case. Let him know his DNA was found on the bunny." Ryan stopped what he was doing and faced her. "I had a look at his car, Andi. No sign of any dents or scratches or paint scuff marks. I wanted to let you know, to put your mind at ease, in case…" His voice trailed off, but she caught his insinuation and her body stiffened.

"You thought it might be him?"

"It crossed my mind. You are divorced, after all. Do you ever see each other?"

She turned away, her heart aching in a way it hadn't in years. "No."

"Was the divorce acrimonious, then?"

"Are you questioning me, Ryan? Is there something you want to say?"

He put down his rag and came closer. "I'm sorry. I know I probably sound blunt. I don't mean to upset you."

She looked into his eyes, so steady and calm and… kind. "How much has Shelby told you?" she asked quietly.

"Nothing, other than saying Jim is a jerk." He smiled faintly. "Which, as your loyal best friend, I would expect."

"I played a big part in our divorce. It wasn't just him." The truth hurt her. She'd tried so hard to be a good wife. A good mother. The accusations he'd flung at her before he walked out had cut her deeply, in wounds that hadn't yet healed. "I'd had a couple of miscarriages before Chelsea was born, and after she came along I... I think I was so focused on her I forgot about my marriage. Then when she died, my grief was so intense—"

"So he walked out?" Ryan's mouth dropped open in dismay. "Andi. You went through the worst loss a person could have. There's no right way to handle that."

"I did counseling. But Jim...he felt like an outsider, I guess, and looking back, I think he might have been right." She looked at Ryan and fought to keep her voice from trembling. "I've never told anyone this except my therapist," she whispered. "But I think Jim, deep down, blames me for Chelsea's death."

"Because you fell asleep."

She nodded. Of course he knew about that; he'd been part of the investigation. "He knew I was sick, left me the cold medication. But I wasn't supposed to fall asleep and leave her alone. He lost his child, too, you know?"

Ryan turned away, and she sensed an agitation in his posture as he snatched up the rag and started wiping again. She waited. He clearly had something on his mind and would speak when he was ready.

It didn't take long.

He abandoned the letter he was wiping away and faced her. "When you're in a marriage, it's for better or worse. You don't bail at the first moment it gets rough, when your partner needs help. Do you remember this verse? 'Two are better than one, because they have a good return for their labor: If either of them falls down, one can help the other up.' Ecclesiastes," he added. "How could he blame you for something that was clearly an accident? Or leave you because your heart had been broken?"

She was touched by his assertion, even if she knew it wasn't quite realistic. "Marriages don't always stand up to the biggest tests," she said quietly. "Jim was right in that I took him for granted and lost myself in my grief. Maybe he walked out, but I wasn't a very good partner to him, either. I need to own that, Ryan. He took a back seat to our daughter."

Ryan stared at her. "Sounds like he was jealous of his own kid. I'm sorry, Andi. I don't mean to make you feel worse. I just…" His cheeks reddened a bit. "I find it hard to imagine you at fault in any of this. You're the kindest, most caring woman I know."

The compliment went straight to her heart and awakened something in her that had been locked away for a very long time. She'd fought a hard battle within herself about blame and forgiveness. She did blame herself for falling asleep that day. At the same time, she knew in her heart that she would never have willfully neglected or abandoned her daughter. It had been completely unintentional. She was fallible, like any other person.

"Thank you for that," she whispered.

"Don't thank me." His jaw tightened. "I was there, remember? I saw what you went through. I felt that pain in here." He touched his fist to his chest. "To know that whoever did this is now tormenting you, bringing this all back up again…" His gaze sharpened. "It's cruel. It's criminal. And I'm going to do whatever is in my power to make sure they're caught and can never hurt you again."

She stepped back a little. He was so forceful in his convictions that she felt at once intimidated by it and, conversely, protected and cherished. What wouldn't she have given seven years ago, to hear that conviction and support come from Jim's lips instead of criticism?

"I'm sorry," he said, quieter now. "It's not my place to dump on your marriage."

"No, you're right," she admitted. "It wasn't as perfect as it seemed, I guess." She remembered Jim's casual yet cutting remarks, always leaving her feeling as if she wasn't good enough. "And regardless, your support means a lot to me. I'll be honest—it's been a bit frightening, dealing with this latest on my own. Feeling like a target in my own house."

He let out a sigh. "You know, I pulled up the old file, looking for something we might have missed. Up until last week, I might have said this case was random. That Chelsea was in the wrong place at the wrong time, that she wandered away and the killer had the perfect opportunity." He hesitated, then picked up his rag and started scrubbing with renewed vigor. "At the time, we ran checks on any previous offenders living in the area. We ran those checks after you found the rabbit, you know. Looking for commonalities. We came up with nothing. Now, with what's happened to you with the car and now the graffiti, my gut says this isn't random at all. Is there anyone you can think of who might have a reason to want to hurt you?"

The question sent a funny feeling, an uneasy turning, from her chest down to her stomach. It was inconceivable that anyone would ever hate her so much that they would take her child, and she told Ryan so. "I just can't understand that kind of hatred, let alone imagine having it directed at me. Who could I have wronged so completely?"

The spray paint was mostly gone on the door now, but a shadow was left behind. Ryan frowned at it. "You're going to need to repaint the door, I'm afraid," he said, dropping his rag. "It came off okay, but you can still see the hint of it."

Just like the worst wounds, she realized. You could work your way through them and heal, but the scars still lay on your heart as a cold reminder of the pain and suffering.

"I'll pick up some paint," she said softly. She could repaint it in an afternoon and no one would ever know the difference. If only everything else could be fixed so easily.

They picked up the rags and the acetone, storing everything carefully inside the garage. "How about some food now?" she asked. "It's the least I can do for your help."

"I wouldn't say no." He smiled then, and her heart took another one of those little leaps.

He followed her inside, and she showed him where the bathroom was so he could wash his hands. When he came out, she was wiping her hands on a towel. "How do you feel about sandwiches and cupcakes?"

"I have very nice feelings about both," he said. "What can I do to help?"

Andi grinned. "Nothing. I picked them up at the bakery earlier, thinking it would be quick and easy."

She went to the fridge and took out the bag of sand-wiches, then put them on plates. Shaved ham, lots of it, on thickly sliced sourdough and with just the right amount of mustard and cheese. Her mouth watered; she hadn't eaten lunch and was ready to dig in.

They sat at the kitchen table with the sandwiches, a dish of carrot sticks and iced water. It was so nice to have someone to eat with rather than being all alone. Ryan's big presence filled the room with his warm voice and laughter. Over the years she'd noticed how hand-some he was, but he was Shelby's brother, after all, and maybe this wasn't supposed to matter, but he was three years younger than she was. Besides, after the end of her marriage, she hadn't wanted to even consider dating.

Now, tonight, they were sitting at her table, and it felt as much like a date as anything ever had, and more ter-rifying than she'd expected. She took a nervous bite of her sandwich and focused on her plate. This was noth-ing more than Shelby putting ideas into her head on her last visit. Ryan wasn't interested. And good thing. She had enough to deal with right now.

She put on water for tea and then presented the cup-cakes with fake enthusiasm. "Ta-da! Thanks to Avery and her gorgeous pastries. Way more beautiful than I could ever make."

"I doubt that." He smiled up at her. "Thank you, Andi. This was delicious."

"You're welcome. And hey, I can bake. But I can't make anything that compares to what she produces."

"You have other talents."

Andi took out two mugs and dropped tea bags into

them. "I suppose." Nerves bubbled up again. Ryan was so kind, so generous. And deserved so much more than a woman who was in the middle of a murder case and had panic attacks every time something happened.

"You're a wonderful nurse, from what I hear. And that can't be easy, dealing with people who are sick or worried they might be sick. It takes a lot of compassion and empathy."

She shrugged. "Most people are great. They just need someone to help it be okay. Occasionally people are not so great. Just like you were saying earlier."

The kettle clicked and she poured the water in the mugs to steep. Outside, the warm fall afternoon had turned to twilight. The days were getting so much shorter now that they were nearly into October.

"You must have some stories." He sat back in his chair and eyed the cupcake. "This almost looks too pretty to eat."

"I eat the frosting off the top first," she said, laughing despite herself. "Then it doesn't look so pretty, and I have no problem digging into the cake."

He lifted the confection, peeled off the wrapper and took a big bite. Cappuccino buttercream stuck to the tip of his nose, and his eyes sparkled above the treat.

"Or there's that way." She took the tea bags out of the mugs and asked, "Milk or sugar?"

"Just a little milk."

They took their tea the same way. Andi reminded herself this was not an important detail or a sign of anything fated. What was wrong with her tonight?

She poured the milk and set the cups on the table.

"There. And in response to your thing about having stories, I have a few."

"Putting my cop hat on for a moment, any that you can think of that were particularly volatile?"

The tea was too hot to drink, so Andi cradled the mug in her hands. "That's a tough question, Ryan. There've been a few, but it's a big leap to go from someone cussing me out in the doctor's office to abducting and murdering my child."

"It is," he said gently, "but not impossible. In the original investigation, you said there was no one. Do you think you'd amend that now? Emotions were so high at the time."

Suddenly the idea of the cupcake wasn't so appealing, and she put it down on her plate. "To say anything feels like me saying I think they're capable of this, and I just can't imagine it."

Ryan broke off a piece of cupcake and put it in his mouth. "Sometimes we just never know. And isn't it worth exploring? Andi, I don't want to see this escalate. I don't want you to get hurt. If there's even a sliver of something, a remote chance, you owe it to yourself and to Chelsea to examine it. If it's nothing, it's nothing. But right now, we haven't got anything other than some black paint from your bumper and some profanity on your garage door. The scene gave us very little, and nothing conclusive. Outdoor scenes are tough at the best of times. Add in the rain of that day and…" He sighed.

"There've been a few over the years," she admitted, feeling on more solid ground now that they were talking about the case. "People who blame the doctors or staff or whoever happens to be in the room at the time for their troubles. We don't take it personally. It's hard when people get a bad diagnosis."

Still. There were a few that stuck in her mind, cases she would never forget. The new bride who was diagnosed with leukemia two months after her wedding. She'd sat in the exam room and cried for a full thirty minutes, breaking Andi's heart. The elderly man whose wife was diagnosed with congestive heart failure and how he'd sat holding her hand the entire time, even as his eyes had filled with tears. But the worst were the miscarriages, which happened more than Andi liked to admit. It was the shattering of a dream each time, and one she felt acutely, having suffered two of her own.

She lifted her gaze and found Ryan studying her, his face kind and patient. "Most people are sad, not angry," she said. "Or their anger comes out in frustration. Only once or twice have I ever had someone be truly vindictive. And who am I to judge? The force of the anger is equal to the force of the pain, in my mind."

"But there was one?"

She nodded, remembering it now, recalling how awful it had been that day. The patient had come straight to the clinic rather than try to get an appointment in the city with their obstetrician. "You understand I can't say anything because of patient confidentiality," she murmured. "But if you get a court order, you can access her records. She blamed the doctor and me for what happened. There were witnesses at the clinic, too."

He sighed. "I get it and I understand. You're quite right that everything has to follow a process."

"You get the paperwork and I'll tell you what I remember," she assured him.

"When did it happen?"

She thought back. "The spring before Chelsea died, I think. April, maybe May. Same year, though, because…"

Her voice trailed away as the memory sneaked in, unwanted. "Because the last thing she said to me was that she hoped I lost my child and then I'd know how it felt."

Chapter Six

Ryan rubbed his eyes and wondered what he was missing.

He was on his third cup of coffee that morning and he was still tired. His mind never seemed to shut off. Going through the old files was a tedious, painstaking job. There'd been so few leads he felt as if he were looking for any little nugget they might have missed. They'd eliminated anyone with a criminal history back then, and the recent cross-referencing had turned up nothing. The close contact list from back then was short—Andi and Jim, naturally, a small circle of family and friends. The idea of it being a random killing seemed unlikely, too, with the reappearance of the rabbit.

His gaze caught on another name, and he jotted it down for follow-up. Leslie Kenney, the twenty-one-year-old babysitter. She'd cared for Chelsea for just over two years. It was a long shot, but he had to be thorough.

Meanwhile, he'd followed up on Andi's former patient. On paper, Roxanne Fletcher looked like a possibility. He'd managed to get her health records and had quickly learned that she'd found out her unborn child was dead in her womb at thirty weeks. He imagined the horror of having to go through the pain of labor without the reward of a healthy baby at the end and knew it was something he would never be able to understand. They'd questioned Andi about it, and she'd been frank about the threats and accusations hurled her way, and she'd also said she was sure Roxanne had nothing to do with Chelsea's murder. He tended to agree with her, but today they were going to talk to Roxanne anyway because he believed in evidence and not gut feelings. Gut feelings didn't stand up in court.

He wasn't the one doing the questioning. Ben was, as lead investigator on the case. Ryan was observing instead. He watched on the monitor as Ben escorted a woman into the room, made sure she had water and took a seat across from her.

Ryan made a mental note of each detail. Thirty-six, according to her file, married, no children. Hmm. No children after the loss of her child. He made a note to check her file again to see if there was a fertility issue. Losing a child and then losing the ability to bear more children was a powerful motivator, especially if you blamed someone. He'd seen many crimes committed for far less.

Roxanne Fletcher looked a little worse for wear. Her jeans were faded and hung on her thin frame, and she wore a Red Deer Rebels sweatshirt that had seen newer days. Her hair was limp, and her skin held a heightened tone that he generally associated with heavy drinking. All in all, his impression was that she'd had a rough life.

Ben asked his questions calmly. What kind of car did she drive? Where had she been last Sunday night? Fletcher looked confused at some of the questions but answered them without getting upset. Eventually, she looked at Ben and drew her brows into a frown. "Why am I here? I don't understand. I didn't do nothing wrong."

Ben took the questions in a different direction, and Ryan leaned closer to the monitor. "Ms. Fletcher, where were you the morning Chelsea Wallace disappeared?"

Her head snapped up, suddenly alert. "Chelsea Wallace? That had to be six years ago or more."

"Seven," Ben replied calmly. "She disappeared on September seventeenth and her body was found on the nineteenth."

"I…I don't remember exactly. I was drinking a lot in those days. I had a job, though. I was cleaning houses with a company based out of town. They closed a few years ago. And I do remember where I was when word came that she'd been found." Roxanne rested her elbows on the table. "I was cleaning out at the Diamond place, helping the older Mrs. Diamond with the heavy fall cleaning."

Ryan sighed. Sam Diamond's mother had passed just last year. She wouldn't be able to corroborate that statement.

"I remember because Clara—Ty's wife—came in with the news. She was crying about it. We all were."

She looked up, right at Ben. "Losing a child is the worst thing in the world. Do you have kids, Officer?"

"I do," Ben answered softly. "And it's fair to say that you know this from personal experience. Am I right?"

She looked away, and Ryan saw her lip quiver. "Yes, sir."

"Did you ever blame anyone for what happened to your baby, Ms. Fletcher?"

She didn't look at him but shook her head quickly.

"You were a patient at the Cadence Creek Medical Clinic. Is that where you found out that your baby had died?" Ben kept his voice soft and sympathetic.

She nodded, then swiped at her eyes.

"Do you remember anything you said on that day?" he asked.

She shook her head again. "I'm sorry, Officer. I don't." She looked up, her face sorrowful, but Ryan thought she looked utterly honest. "I know I yelled at some people. It was the worst news in the world. I kind of lost it. I still don't understand what that has to do with anything."

"Do you remember threatening anyone?"

"No, sir, I swear I don't."

"You don't remember—" he checked his file in front of him and then looked back up "—saying you hoped the nurse lost the most important thing in her life so she'd know how it felt?"

Roxanne Fletcher paled. "I said that?"

"According to witnesses, yes."

"That nurse…that was Andi Wallace." Her mouth dropped open and she pushed back from the table. "You don't think I have anything to do with her little girl's murder, do you?" She started to cry. "That's so cruel. I could never hurt a child. Never deprive a mother of her baby. I know I lashed out, but I swear it was just that. Lashing out. Not…" She looked up at him. "I think I'm gonna be sick."

Ben stood and quickly got her a trash can, and she vomited in it.

Ryan sat back and rubbed his index finger along his chin. That was an interesting response. It was true that the idea might be so repulsive that she was physically ill, but it was also possible that she was so afraid of finally being caught that it made her sick. Her face had taken on a strange sheen, and he wondered if she was sweating.

"Ms. Fletcher, I'm just trying to put some pieces together. If you can give me some names I can follow up with, I'm sure this'll be cleared up in no time."

She nodded quickly. "Of course. I'll do what I can to help."

Ryan watched until the interview was over and then went to find Ben. "What do you think?" he asked, standing in the older man's office door.

"I've got some follow-up to do to confirm her whereabouts. She does have a black car, and her husband has been working up north in the oil patch, so she's been home alone. Lots of opportunity."

Ryan nodded. "It's the first real lead we've had in years. We never had any sort of motive before."

"Funny Andi didn't mention it at the time."

"Stress and panic? I don't know. I think it's good to follow it through, though."

"Me, too."

Ben sat back in his chair. "This case was the hardest one of my career so far. We're a small town, small detachment. We see our share, but not little girls…" He swallowed, his throat bobbing. "I know how I would have felt if that had been Susie. I can understand Andi's mind going blank. There's no space for anything but worry and panic."

Ryan knew that Ben was a dedicated father. He was married to a lawyer, Camilla, and she had become stepmother to Ben's daughter, Susie, and then mom to two boys. The three kids kept Ben busy…and, Ryan thought, balanced.

Family had a way of doing that. Maybe that was why Shelby and his folks were always after him to settle down. Lately it seemed his whole life revolved around work.

He pushed the thoughts aside. He went to the coffee maker and poured two cups, then took them both back into Ben's office. They could go through the interview notes together. Somewhere there had to be a telltale clue they were missing.

Three hours later Ryan didn't feel any further ahead. "Hey, Ben, did we ever look into the babysitter? Leslie?"

Ben rubbed a hand over his chin. "Yes, briefly. But she was twenty-one and frantic that Chelsea was missing. There was no motive there, either." Ben frowned. "But I'll admit we didn't look at her very closely."

This could be the gap, the bit that had been over-looked. "Mind if I do some checking?" Ryan asked.

"Not at all. It's worth a shot."

Ryan poured himself another cup of coffee and sat at his desk. As far as he was concerned, he had one job to do, and that was to find out who was targeting Andi.

On Sunday, Ryan was pleasantly surprised to see Andi at church again. She looked tired, but so very pretty in a rust-red dress and black heels as she spoke to an older couple at the sanctuary door. She accepted her bulletin and once again sat at the back of the congregation. Someone spoke to her, and her smile was a beacon on an otherwise cloudy October morning.

Next week would be Thanksgiving Sunday, he realized. His parents would be hosting the entire family for a massive turkey dinner. Would it be unprofessional of him to ask Andi along? Could it be construed as a date? He frowned. He shouldn't invite her, not when the investigation was still open. He needed to keep his head clear and his heart uninvolved. It was getting harder and harder to do, though, when she was everywhere he turned, looking at him with her soft eyes and wistful smile.

"Uncle Ry!" Carson came bumping along, grabbing on to Ryan's arm as he tripped on his shoelace.

Ryan hoisted him up and held him on his arm, even though Carson was getting far too big to do so. "Nice tie, dude," he said to the boy, who was wearing his Sunday white shirt and a cute little red clip-on tie.

"You're not wearing one. Mama says we have to wear a tie to church."

"I wore a sweater instead. No collar for me to put a tie."

Carson looked him dead in the eye. "You're gonna be in trouble, Uncle Ry."

He laughed. How could he not? His little nephew was adorable. And also heavy. He put him down. "You'd better tie your laces. Your mama surely has something to say about that."

"She does. She says I'll trip and knock out a tooth."

He laughed again. It seemed everywhere he turned this week there were signs of the joys and fulfillment of parenthood. He was thirty-two. Maybe it was time he considered settling down.

His gaze fell on Andi again. At that moment she looked over and their eyes met. She smiled, and he felt it right down to his toes.

There was still time before the service started, so he slid into the pew beside her. "It's nice to see you back."

She shrugged. "I almost didn't come. God and I aren't on the greatest of terms right now."

He understood and would never judge. "So why did you?"

"I don't know, really. I'm… Oh, let's not get into this right now. Is that okay?"

"Of course it is." They'd both kept their voices down, but Ryan smiled and raised his a little to a normal volume. "Do you have Thanksgiving plans next weekend?" he asked.

She looked slightly startled. "Oh. I, uh, don't know.

My folks are on vacation, so I won't be going to Calgary."

"Mom and Dad are having everyone at their place. I'm sure one more is no bother." He toyed with his bulletin and realized his hands were starting to sweat. "I mean, you're like one of the family anyway."

The light in her eyes dimmed a bit, but her smile held steady. "I'll think about it," she replied.

He moved on and took his seat with Shelby and her family. He got sight of Andi once more, as she shook hands with the minister and made a beeline for her car.

It was no use. He was starting to think of her as more than a friend. And that worried him, because she was in danger, and he needed to keep his wits about him.

Andi tried to relax on the drive home from church, but she wasn't having much luck. The lack of sleep was getting to her, she supposed. She had a hard time falling asleep, and then she was restless all night, sometimes waking up several times. She felt on the verge of another panic attack all the time and had started having nightmares about the day Chelsea disappeared. She was really not okay and didn't want anyone to know it.

The police had come up with nothing so far. Nothing on the stuffed animal or from the scene, or her car, or the tagging of her garage door. Her breath never quite seemed to fill her lungs anymore; it was shallow with anxiety, wondering what was going to happen next. If it was going to escalate into something threatening her physically. Not sleeping, not feeling safe… It was hard to fake being okay.

But she'd done her level best at church because she didn't want Shelby to hover, and she didn't want to look weak in front of Ryan.

Besides, she knew what he'd say. They were doing all they could. Maybe they were, but what if that wasn't good enough?

The air had a distinct bite to it when she got out of her car and headed to her house. The day stretched out, long and lonely, and she was dreading it. Too much time to think, to worry, to miss the life she'd once had.

"Stop feeling sorry for yourself," she said firmly, unlocking the front door. She had a good life despite her losses. Whatever was happening now would pass. She should be counting her blessings instead.

She put her purse on the bench by the front door and hung her coat on the hook above it, then put her keys on the tinier hook installed for just that purpose. Jim had always chided her for losing track of her keys, in one pocket or another, a different purse, on the counter. He'd put the hook in to make it easier. She frowned. Somehow she resented that. She could put her keys anywhere she wanted. She plucked them off the hook and put them on the kitchen counter, then stared at them for a full ten seconds before putting them back on the hook again, laughing a little at herself. Truthfully, the hook was the best place for them. She was just on edge. Had been for days.

A cup of tea would help. She flipped on the kettle and grabbed the tin of tea bags out of the cupboard, plopping one in the bottom of a mug. Then she went to her room to change out of her dress and into something more comfortable. A pair of yoga pants and a soft fleecy hoodie sounded perfect. As she pulled the sweatshirt over her head, she thought about Jim again and how he'd never liked it when she wore what he called "stretchy pants." He'd always liked to see her dressed up when she wasn't in scrubs and had called her his pretty girl. She'd liked that. Being called *pretty* by her husband. But now that she was alone, she also liked being able to wear yoga pants if she wanted.

Why was she thinking about Jim so much today, anyway? They were long over. Maybe because she'd been spending time with Ryan? She'd definitely been noticing him. She supposed it was natural to think back on old relationships when… She let out a sigh. When she was thinking about someone new all the time.

She hadn't cared what Ryan thought when he came over to help the other day. She'd worn her rattiest clothes and it had been absolutely fine. She was so comfortable with him. When she started to consider why that might be, the thoughts got overwhelming, so she pushed them aside. For now.

She was nearly back to the kitchen when she noticed the photo sitting on the dining table.

It was one of Chelsea, not long after she was born, sitting in her carrier, wearing an adorable dress with ruffled bottoms over her diaper and a huge smile on her face. She hadn't had much hair then, and it was blond and wispy, but her eyes had been wide and laughing. Andi reached out to touch it, to pick it up, her fingers trembling. Her baby girl… Oh, she'd been so precious. Remembering her this way made her heart ache with an emptiness she knew would never go away. It was true what they said. Days got easier, but you never, ever got over losing a child.

It wasn't until Andi had the photo in her hand that realization struck her with a sharp stab of dread. This photo…it wasn't from any of the few that were framed and displayed in the house. This one was from an album. And all the albums were tucked away in a chest in Chelsea's old room.

The kettle clicked off, but Andi ignored it and went to the table to sit down. She was so tired. So stressed. But she would remember going through an album, wouldn't she? She wouldn't forget doing something like that. She put her forehead on her hand. Was she losing her mind? This time of year was always hard, but with the threats, she knew she really wasn't coping well. The thought that she might be having gaps in her memory freaked her out.

The only other alternative was that someone else had been here and left it. Someone had been in her home. It seemed impossible, but a week ago she wouldn't have imagined being nearly run off the road or having her garage painted with obscenities, either. She squared her shoulders and let out a breath, trying to find her logic. Someone was playing mind games with her. She was certain she hadn't forgotten going into the room and taking out a picture.

Her pulse raced as she went to Chelsea's room and opened the door. It no longer had her daughter's things in it. After a few years, Andi had considered it un-healthy to keep it as a memorial, and she'd packed up her daughter's things and donated them to charity, while keeping items with sentimental value. They'd all gone into a sweet wooden chest that her dad had built for Chelsea before she was born. The rest of the room was now decorated as a spare room, but as Andi entered it, she remembered it as it had been. Walls of a pink so pale it reminded her of the inside of an apple blossom. A white crib that they'd converted into a toddler bed that last summer, with a white dresser and a change table. And stuffed animals... So many stuffed animals, teddies and bunnies and little lambs. Pink-and-white gingham curtains over the window blind, filtering the morning sunlight. Andi had loved walking into this room in the morning, with the sun shining and her baby girl's face just as sunny and happy.

The chest sat in the corner, and Andi went and knelt before it. Her body was so full of anxiety that her breath was shallow and her muscles tight, but she made herself open the lid and look inside.

It still smelled of baby lotion and an essence that was little girl, something soft and sweet mingled with the scent of faded paper. She took a few precious minutes to just absorb the scent and the beautiful memories it evoked. When she was finally ready, she looked down into the chest. Nothing looked amiss, not a single thing. She lifted out the blanket Jim's grandmother had quilted for Chelsea and put it aside carefully, then took out a teddy bear and a christening gown that Andi had worn as a baby and that Chelsea had also worn to her baptism. Beneath all of it were two photo albums. Andi had eschewed keeping all the photos on a hard drive and had instead printed her favorites out, putting them in albums with cute little scrapbook stickers and captions. Her hands shook as she took out the first one and began turning the pages.

Oh, the memories. Sweet and devastating all at once. How happy she'd looked, a new mother with her tiny baby in her arms. And Jim, too, though he rarely ever smiled when he was getting his picture taken. They'd been a family, though, doing things together. Or so she'd thought. As she looked at the photos now, she knew he'd felt left out. Felt as if she'd only had eyes for her baby and no longer for her husband. Was it true? She didn't think so. She looked back on how hard she'd tried to be a good mother but also a good wife. Maybe it was just as she'd told Ryan—sometimes marriages didn't withstand the toughest tests.

She kept flipping, remembering each moment, until she turned a page and there—a photo was missing. It was the one she'd found, with a handwritten sticker above the empty space that said, "Four-month checkup and big smiles!"

She hadn't been in this chest. She hadn't. She would have remembered coming in here and having to dig through the contents to find the albums. But someone had. And they'd taken the photo out and left it for her to find.

Someone had been in her house. Someone who knew where to look. The list was not a long one.

She put down the album and sat on her bottom, unsure of what to do. She hadn't felt safe before, but now she felt…violated. And scared. Whoever was doing these things was trying to frighten her. Trying to make her feel off-balance and unclear. She thought back to the conversation she'd had with Ryan about Roxanne Fletcher. As a nurse, she understood that what Roxanne had gone through—being told her baby was dead—was severely traumatic. But was it traumatic enough for her to still blame Andi after so many years? She scoured her brain for any other person she could think of who would be so twisted they would want to punish her again. Wasn't the first time enough? There'd been patients who'd been rude. What had she missed? Had she inadvertently done someone harm? But still… Who would know where to find a photo album? She looked around the room. She supposed it wasn't that much of a long shot. The chest was the one thing out of place, the one thing that was still childish in the redecorated space, with handles shaped like little duckies and Chelsea's name just under the hasp.

Today was a turning point for her. Enough was enough. They were several steps behind whoever this was, and it was time they caught up. She wasn't losing her mind. If the person who had put this photo on her table had thought it would make her doubt herself, thought it would terrify her, they were wrong. Oh, she was scared. But the longer this went on, the angrier she got. It was time she channeled that anger into action.

She thought back to the day in the woods when she ran through the trees in pursuit of what turned out to be a deer, but she'd thought it was the perpetrator. She'd been a bit foolish, granted, but she needed to channel that mama-bear feeling.

She got up from the floor, went to the kitchen and got her purse. She tucked the photo inside, grabbed her keys and locked the door behind her as she stepped into the chilly afternoon. The time for waiting for answers was over. It was time to go find them instead.

Chapter Seven

When Andi opened the door to the Cadence Creek detachment and stepped inside, every head swiveled in her direction.

She stopped at the window and spoke to the officer on duty. Ryan knew right away that something had happened. Not just because of the determined set of her lips, but because she was actually here, at the station. She didn't like it here. Didn't like dealing with the police, which he understood. The last time she'd been inside the detachment, she'd been grilled about her daughter's disappearance and made to feel as if it was her fault. So for her to be here today meant something new had happened.

The officer rose from his chair and came around the corner to where Ryan waited. "Mrs. Wallace is here to see Sergeant Rogers."

"He's off today."

"I know. I asked if she needed to make a report and she said she wanted to speak to him about her case."

The young officer shrugged. "I can make her an appointment for tomorrow."

But it had to be something important for her to come all the way in here. "Bring her in. I'll talk to her. If she still needs to see Ben, we'll set it up."

The officer led Andi to an empty office, where she sat and put her purse on her lap. She was wound pretty tight, he realized, watching from a distance. Before going in, he filled two cups with coffee and fixed hers with a little sugar and milk. He needed her to relax.

"Andi. This is a surprise. I hear you came to see Ben."

She turned around at the sound of his voice and her brow wrinkled. "Is he here?"

"Not until tomorrow. Will I do?"

She sighed. "Don't take this the wrong way, but you're not the lead investigator."

"No, I'm not."

"And I'm done messing around."

He was glad to hear the strength and determination in her voice. He put the coffee in front of her and kept his body loose, his tone conversational. "I can tell you're frustrated. Did something else happen?"

Her gaze met his, and fire blazed behind the brown depths of her eyes. Whatever had propelled her here had set her off in a big way.

She reached into her handbag and pulled out a photo, then placed it on the table. He picked it up. It was Chelsea, he assumed, as a little baby, looking cute and adorable. He looked away from the picture and into her face again. "I'm assuming something happened with the picture?"

She nodded. "This photo is kept in an album at the bottom of a chest in Chelsea's old room. When I got home from church today, it was sitting on the dining table." She looked up at him meaningfully. "I didn't put it there."

He slid into the seat across the desk from her.

"I didn't. I know you're probably thinking I just don't remember, or the stress is getting to me and I've cracked, but I'm telling you. I did not take this picture out of the album."

He didn't for a moment think she'd "cracked." Was she under stress? Sure. But she'd been bearing up remarkably well, in his opinion. "To clarify, you're saying someone else did."

"Someone was in my house, Ryan. Someone got that photo out of the album and left it there for me. It was bad enough when they were on my property and vandalized my garage. But now they've been in my home." There was an edge of anger in her voice that he hadn't heard before. She'd said she was done messing around, and he believed her.

He understood how violated she must feel right now, and vulnerable, knowing someone had been in her space. Her words about not remembering also told him something else: at some point, someone had made her doubt herself. Had made her question her own logic and memory. She'd answered the question before he even had a chance to ask it. She hadn't forgotten and she hadn't broken down. Even now, she was upset but steady and certain.

He looked at her and frowned. "And now we've both had our hands on the photo. Any fingerprints that might have been on it are probably ruined."

Her face fell. "I never thought of that."

He should have. He let the silence spill out into the room for several seconds before he asked what he'd been wanting to ask for two weeks.

"Andi, what was your relationship like with Jim?"

Her head snapped up. "You can't think that he did this. Our marriage ended badly, but I can't imagine he'd do something like this." Her mouth worked for a moment before she said, quieter, "For him to have the stuffed rabbit after all this time... I can put two and two together, Ryan. This means you're also asking if he could have killed Chelsea. You're insinuating he was capable of murdering his own child." There was disbelief and disgust in every word. "No."

He took a breath, reminding himself to go gently. "I know it sounds harsh. Statistically, though, most murders of children are perpetrated by a parent."

"Like what kind of statistic?" She looked up, her eyes curious.

"The last number I saw put it around 90 percent."

She let out her breath in a whoosh. "That's so horrible. I just... I can't imagine that." Her eyes searched his. "What is wrong with people?"

"I ask myself that a lot." Sometimes it was hard not to turn into a cynic. He picked up his coffee and took a sip, trying to ease the atmosphere a little more.

She mirrored his movement, and he noticed her shoulders dropped a little. Good.

"All right. So back to the photo. When did you notice it?"

"About half an hour ago, when I went to check the album."

"You didn't notice it missing from the album before that?"

"No."

"And when was the last time you looked at your albums?"

She frowned. "I don't know. A long time."

"Days?" he asked. "Weeks, months?"

"Maybe a year and a half ago," she admitted.

"So the photo could have been taken anytime between a year ago April and, well, today."

"Yes." She sighed. "I didn't think of that, either." After a moment she brightened. "But it still means someone was in my house. They would have had to have been to put it there today."

He nodded. "And you said the albums were in a chest."

"I keep all her things there for safekeeping."

His heart turned over at the wistfulness that permeated Andi's voice. He reached over and touched her hand. "I know this is so difficult for you. I'm sorry."

She nodded and took another drink of what he knew was questionable coffee. "The location isn't a secret, but the albums aren't out in the open, either. A person would have to go looking."

"And know what to look for. Or have substantial time to search around."

Andi bit down on her lip. "I'm tired, Ryan. Someone is playing these games with me, threatening me. For a moment today I actually did wonder if I'd taken out the picture and somehow forgotten about it. After Chelsea disappeared, I often had these feelings of... I don't know. Not being present, not having my head in the right place. I'd forget things, which I put down to stress and, well, lack of sleep. For a moment today I had that same lost feeling, and it made me so angry. I didn't take this out and forget about it, though. I didn't."

"I believe you." The words were easy to say because they were true. All the events to this point had been designed to play mind games with Andi.

Ryan thought back to his earlier idea. "So the people who would know, you said it was a short list. You, your ex-husband, your parents, I'd guess. Anyone else? Anyone who provided childcare or babysat now and again?"

"Yes to all of those, I guess. The people most often in our house were the two of us and Leslie, our babysitter. We didn't have to take Chelsea to day care. Leslie came to us. We were very lucky."

"Have you seen her lately?"

"No. But she'd be what, twenty-seven by now? Maybe twenty-eight. I doubt she's been nearby for years."

Mentally he started building a list.

"I can't imagine Leslie having anything to do with this. She was so shattered when Chelsea died. So frantic." A shadow passed over Andi's face. "She blamed me, too, at the time. Said that I should have called her to look after Chelsea when I was sick and couldn't care for my own child."

Her gaze held Ryan's. "People say things when they're overwrought."

"Yes," he agreed, "they do."

Andi lifted her coffee cup, but Ryan could see her fingers shake a little now.

"Let's get back to Jim for a moment. Did he ever say things that made you doubt yourself or your recollection of things that happened?"

Her jaw tightened. He could tell she really didn't like this line of questioning, but they were still checking out Roxanne's alibis and he had to examine all angles. If he could just figure out a motive…

"Sometimes," she whispered. "I mean, I did forget a lot. I was always losing things. He'd tease me about it. Like my keys. He put in this hook so I'd never misplace them again. Then he'd say stuff like, 'Good thing you have me around to keep things straight,' and stuff like that." She shrugged, but he noticed she looked smaller in her chair.

"And since you divorced, have you had trouble finding your keys? Are you disorganized at work?"

"No, of course not!" She laughed a little. "I have to keep things organized and documented at work."

"Why did you divorce, anyway?" he asked, keeping his voice as gentle as possible. "I know you said Chelsea's death was hard, but was there more?"

He watched as she swallowed, evaded his eyes. He waited patiently. He had almost given up on her saying anything when she said in a small voice, "He said he couldn't compete for my attention when Chelsea was alive, and now that she was gone, he couldn't compete with her ghost. That he…" Her voice broke a little and she took a breath. "That he deserved better. That I couldn't do anything right, and it was all my fault. That I was a failure as a wife and as a mother, too."

Ryan sat back, stunned that she'd actually admitted all that, angry that anyone would say those things to her and positive that none of it was true. What he did have, though, was the beginning of a motive. Jealousy could be a dangerous emotion. Perhaps they needed to be taking a closer look at Jim Wallace.

Andi couldn't believe she'd actually admitted the truth of her marital breakdown. It was, next to falling asleep the day of Chelsea's disappearance, her biggest failure. And she'd tried so hard. Tried everything to make Jim happy, to make him look at her again the way he had when they'd been dating. Like she was his heaven, moon and stars.

Ryan reached across the desk and laced his fingers with hers. "You are not a failure at either of those things," he said, and there was a tenderness in his voice that reached inside and soothed. "I promise you, Andi. You are not. You're an incredible woman, who has been through so much. You came in here today like a mama bear. I like that woman a lot."

She nodded, trying to keep tears at bay. The unconditional support made her as emotional as reopening old wounds.

"Our marriage was a mess, I think," she admitted.

"I wasn't happy, even when I told myself I was. All the little digs just ate away at me."

"It happened a lot?"

"More than I've ever wanted to admit." She had spent ages trying to explain away all the things Jim said and did. He was tired from working, he missed her, he'd had a bad day... But the truth was he'd whittled away at her bit by bit, and then he'd apologize and tell her he loved her and was just trying to help.

"Have you heard of the term *gaslighting*?" Ryan kept his fingers twined with hers, and she was glad for the link, even if it was inappropriate. "It's a kind of psychological manipulation that makes you doubt your own recall, your abilities, your self-esteem. It might be worth looking into, because it sounds as if your relationship with Jim wasn't exactly healthy."

She knew he was right, but it was so hard to admit it. Besides, she wasn't perfect. She'd made tons of mistakes. She pulled her hand away from Ryan's and rested her forehead on it. Oh, good grief. This was it, wasn't it? Her self-esteem had gone into the toilet when she'd been married to Jim, and it had improved in the years since but had never quite come back.

"I think I probably need more therapy." She looked up at him, feeling utterly miserable. "I tackled a lot of the grief, but not our relationship and divorce. Oh, I can't believe I've told you all this today. I'm so sorry. You don't need my marital baggage."

"It's all right. I'm a police officer but I'm also your friend." He smiled a little. "If that's okay."

"Of course it's okay. I wouldn't have called you that first day otherwise."

Warmth settled around them, and then Ryan cleared his throat. "Okay, so first things first. We need to figure out who's doing this and put a stop to it. Your safety is the biggest priority right now."

"You believe me about the picture."

"Yes, I do. But I hate that he played you to the point where you doubt yourself and others' ability to see what's right in front of them."

"What do you mean?"

He sighed. "Let's put a pin in that for another day. Instead, let's talk about ensuring your safety. Did you have your locks changed after Jim moved out?"

"He gave me the keys back," she said. It only took a moment before her face cleared and she raised one eyebrow. "Okay, going with your thought process here, I'm guessing you're thinking he could have made a copy, no problem."

"It crossed my mind. Did Leslie also have keys?"

"Yes. But—"

"It doesn't necessarily mean anything, just that there are keys to your place out there. Did you notice any signs of forced entry?"

She shook her head. Not that she'd known exactly what to look for. But nothing stood out.

"You should have a locksmith come out and change your locks. We'll double-check your windows, too. It's Sunday, so the locks won't happen today, but we can get that done for you tomorrow. Tonight, I think you should stay somewhere else, just as a precaution."

She hoped he didn't suggest his place. They were friends, perhaps a little bit more, but staying with him, even if she slept on the sofa, would be so inappropriate.

"I can call Shelby. I do have to work tomorrow, so driving to my folks' place isn't really ideal."

"Good plan. We can set up cameras, too, if you want."

She thought about the cost of all that and frowned. "I don't have a huge budget, Ryan. I have a good job but also have the sole responsibility of the expenses."

"No alimony?"

She shook her head. "I never asked for any." Then she met his eyes. "I know. It was stupid."

"Not stupid," he contradicted. "Misguided, perhaps. And kind. Probably more than he deserved."

She ignored that jab at Jim. "We split everything else down the middle," she said. "And then he moved farther north and that was that. Anyway, about the cameras. It's a good idea but I just don't know. It feels so strange even having this conversation."

"Let me do some digging, see what it would cost," he said. "But locks for sure."

Andi was quiet for a few moments, coming to terms with what this conversation meant. It was so big, so unreal, that she was having trouble coming to grips with it all. "I'm sorry, Ryan. This is just so hard for me. He was my husband and her father. Even considering he could be behind this is hard to wrap my head around. If he did this, what part did I play in it? Why couldn't I see what was right in front of me?"

Andi knew that question would haunt her for the rest

of her days. It was better to just believe it was someone else. For her sake, she hoped the evidence led them in a different direction.

Of course Shelby agreed to let Andi stay the night, and after the kids had gone to bed and the two women sat down for a cup of mint tea, Andi told Shelby everything that had been happening. She didn't tell her about the part of the conversation that centered around Jim. She wasn't quite ready to delve into that more deeply today. Besides, she'd had time to think after leaving the detachment, and the idea that Jim had anything to do with this was ludicrous. Jim had been by her side the whole time. He was the one who'd come home from work and discovered Chelsea was missing. He'd shared in her grief, not caused it. He had his faults, but a murderer? She had the same thoughts about Leslie. Good heavens, Leslie had loved Chelsea as if she were her own. Andi had never known a gentler, more loving soul.

She slept on the pullout sofa and was up and in her scrubs and ready for work, the bed made back up, by seven thirty the next morning. Shelby was already up looking after the kids and getting Ian out the door to work. Normally Andi just grabbed a coffee before work and ate later, but Shelby sat her down and plied her with scrambled eggs and toast. Then it was the rush to get Carson out the door to catch the school bus. As Andi watched the commotion, she missed it all desperately. She would have had that with Chelsea, and she'd wanted more children. Knowing she would never have any now sent a dull ache through her stomach.

"Okay." Shelby let out a long breath. "Carson and Ian are out the door. Macy's had as much breakfast as I can get into her, and now it's just you, me and Gilly." She grinned at the one-year-old sitting in the high chair, picking up Cheerios with her fist and shoving them in her mouth. "Okay, lovely, you need some fruit to go with those oats."

Andi spread homemade strawberry jam on her toast and watched as Shelby spooned mashed bananas into Gillian's mouth. "She's a good eater."

"All three of them are. I'm a little afraid of when they become teenagers. Ian just shrugs and says, 'The Lord provides.'"

Andi smiled. "You have a wonderful family, you know. Thank you for letting me stay last night."

"You can stay as long as you need," Shelby decreed.

"It's okay. Ryan's having someone change my locks today."

Shelby focused on scooping up more banana. "You and Ryan have been spending a lot of time together."

"We've become friends, I think. Not just because he's your brother, but friends all on our own. He's been really helpful," she said. And then added, "And he believes me."

"I'm afraid for you, Andi." Shelby frowned. "I'm glad Ryan is looking out for you. And I've been praying for this to come to a resolution soon. I want you safe and able to put this behind you."

Andi knew it would never be totally behind her, but she also understood Shelby's meaning. "Me, too. Something's got to break soon." She just hoped it wasn't her.

"Whoever it is will make a mistake. There'll be a clue that can't be ignored." Shelby sounded confident, and Andi wanted to be, but so far there'd been very little to go on.

Once again, she debated telling Shelby about her conversation with Ryan regarding Jim, but something made her hold back. It was just…a lot. And part of that, she realized, was having to acknowledge that if it were possible, she'd missed so many signs and been so wrong.

"I've got to get to work. Thank you for the bed and for breakfast." She smiled as she got up from the table and leaned over and kissed her friend's cheek. "You're a good bestie."

"So are you." Shelby looked up at her with worried eyes. "Please be careful."

"I am," she replied. But life had to go on, so she said goodbye to the kids and headed into town to work. The normality of the morning with Shelby and the kids had been great, but now the pit of dread in her stomach opened up. She had no idea what was coming next, and she wasn't sure how long she could take the uncertainty and fear.

Chapter Eight

Andi's morning was filled with patients, and she didn't get a chance to eat until nearly one o'clock. Since she'd stayed at Shelby's, she hadn't packed a lunch, so she thought she'd treat herself to a take-out treat from the Wagon Wheel café in town. She only had a half hour, so she hurried out the clinic door and straight to her car, her phone pressed to her ear as she waited to put in her order so it would be ready by the time she arrived.

Someone had answered the phone and she was about to give her order when she stopped short. *Not again.*

All her tires were flat. She walked around the car, then crouched by one and saw the slash in the tire wall. It was broad daylight! Whoever was doing this was getting more and more confident, or careless, depending on the perspective. Four tires. This didn't just add to the intimidation—it was going to cause her financial issues. The tow plus four brand-new tires installed? She was going to be out several hundred dollars. Add that to the cost of the new locks today and her credit card was taking a beating.

She was fretting about money, she realized, when the important thing was her safety. The first few incidents were days apart. Now they were getting closer together. It was as if this person was saying "I can get to you anywhere, at any time." She shivered.

"Hello? Are you still there?"

Andi suddenly remembered she was on a call. She stood and rolled her shoulders. "I'm so sorry. I won't be able to place an order after all."

They ended the call and Andi stood there, dumbfounded, trying to make sense of all of this. She looked around the parking lot but saw no one suspicious. A woman left her car and made her way into the dollar store; another with a toddler holding her hand came out of the drugstore. Regular foot traffic, but had anyone seen anything? It could have happened anytime in the last four and a half hours.

Ryan would want to know. She felt needy calling him again, but this was an ongoing investigation and one more thing to add to the list of, at the very least, harassment. She didn't want to feel insecure, unsafe and scared, but she couldn't really help it. This person had been in her house, monitoring her movements, following her to work. She walked around, feeling as if there were eyes constantly watching her. Eventually the stress of that was going to wear her down. That was probably the point, she thought.

She dialed Ryan's cell rather than the detachment. He was off today, supervising the installation of her locks.

It was so above and beyond his duty as an officer. She tried not to read too much into it, but it was difficult. There was something between them. Whether it was solely precipitated by the situation in which she found herself, she wasn't sure. Was it genuine? It wasn't just relying on him that was bothering her. It was how much she looked forward to seeing him. How things seemed to fall into place whenever he was around. He walked in and her heart beat a little faster, and at the same time she felt safe.

He picked up, voice cheerful and light. "Hey, Andi. Checking in on the locksmith?"

She hated that she had to answer, "Not quite. I'm sorry, Ryan. It looks as though my tires have been slashed."

"You're kidding. Wow. This guy's getting brazen."

"Or woman."

"Right." She heard him heave a sigh. "Listen, I'm going to be done in about ten minutes. The guys are just finishing up and I thought I'd go to the hardware and get you an extra key made. I can pop by the clinic first, though."

"I can call the detachment if you need me to. You've done so much off the clock already."

"Let me stop by first and have a look, okay? Is this going to be a problem for you with work?"

She knew it wouldn't be. Dr. Gonzales was a wonderful boss and would work around her absence if she had to leave. It would create more work for the staff still inside, though, particularly without a nurse, and she hated inconveniencing her coworkers. This situation was starting to affect her work and that was even more frustrating. If someone was trying to upend her life, they were doing a great job.

"They'll be fine with it. I need to go back in and tell them what happened."

"I'll be there as soon as I can."

She hung up and turned around, preparing to go back inside and explain to the staff about her extended lunch break, when she noticed a man coming across the parking lot toward her.

Not just any man.

Jim.

Her heart beat out a warning rhythm, and anxiety slithered from her chest down her legs. Ryan's suspicion flooded her mind as he came closer. Unbidden, a horrific scene unfolded in her mind of that awful September day, imagining what might have happened at his hands. She shuddered and pushed it away. No. She and Jim had had their problems, but she would not believe this of him. He'd loved Chelsea. She knew that without a doubt.

Within seconds she was face-to-face with her ex-husband.

"Andi, are you okay?"

She would not let him see her fear and uncertainty. "Oh, I'm fine." She tried a smile and felt it came out weak. "My tires, not so much."

He looked the same as ever. Pressed khakis, button-down shirt, casual leather shoes. His hair was a little on the long side, she noticed, and he looked tired. There was a strain in his face, too, tightening the muscles. He knelt down by a tire and whistled. "Wow. Someone was a real jerk to do that. Do you need me to call you a tow?"

"No, thank you." His easy tone had her completely off-balance. Just moments ago, she'd been wondering if he was capable of the things Ryan had suggested, and now he was in front of her, being friendly and helpful. Which was the real Jim? Her fingers tightened on the strap of her purse. "I can manage just fine." She lifted her chin a little. "I've got help on the way already."

"If you're sure." He stood and rested his weight on one hip, a stance she remembered well. A sense of familiarity washed over her, but it was marred by the memory of him walking out on them and their marriage, and the nasty and hurtful things he'd said.

"I'm positive. You must need to get back to work anyway." She didn't ask what brought him to Cadence Creek. She wasn't sure she wanted to know the answer. Though as a farm equipment salesman, of course he ended up at local businesses and ranches. He had as much right to be here as anyone.

"I can wait with you until the tow comes. Make sure everything goes okay."

The last thing she wanted was for him to come face-to-face with Ryan. And she hadn't called a tow; she'd only said help was on the way. "I really don't want to keep you. I'm sure you want to finish your workday so you can go home."

He shrugged. "Not a big deal when you go home to an empty house. But then, you'd know the feeling."

The words were said casually, but there was a dig in there, as well. Subtle, but just that little edge of nastiness that was also familiar and, now that they weren't married, recognizable for what it was. A jab at her being alone. Chipping away at her happiness and any contentment she might have found without him.

She wished he would just leave.

Just her luck—she wasn't sure if it was good or bad—that Ryan's truck turned into the parking lot. He was forever being prompt, wasn't he?

Her anxiety kicked up another notch.

He pulled up in the spot next to her. She saw his gaze light on Jim and then back to her, questioning, but then he hopped out of the half-ton and his face took on a generic pleasant expression. His cop expression, she realized. This was more than awkward. To her, this felt like a powder keg just waiting for someone to light a match.

"Hey," he said easily, rounding the hood of her car. "Wow. All four." He looked up and kept his posture relaxed, shoulders down, palms slightly out and open. "Hi, Jim. What're you doing here?"

"I was just at the dollar store and noticed Andi here. Came over to say hi and saw the tires. Jerk move, slashing them like that."

"You're telling me." Ryan looked at Andi and his gaze searched hers. "You're okay, though?"

She nodded. "I'm fine." She understood the subtext. He wanted to know if Jim had been threatening or if she was afraid, and she was saying that she was okay and not in danger. At least, she didn't think she was. Maybe it was just Ryan putting ideas into her head, but despite the awkwardness, she was profoundly glad he was there with her now.

Ryan nodded and looked back at Jim. "So what'd you get at the dollar store?" He'd noticed what Andi had not: Jim didn't have a shopping bag.

"Oh, they didn't have what I wanted. It's no big deal. I was just killing time until my next appointment."

"Well, we don't want to keep you," Andi said brightly. "Do we, Ryan?"

Jim's gaze swept from her to Ryan, and then back to her again. She didn't think his expression changed, but there was a new tension in the air that hadn't been there before. Was it because she'd used the term "we"? Was Jim jealous? That was ridiculous. He'd left her six years ago. And she knew for a fact he'd had at least one girlfriend since their split.

"We sure don't." Ryan smiled again.

"So you two are a thing now?"

Despite everything, all her misgivings and doubts, Andi wasn't about to let Jim cross this boundary. "That's really none of your business, is it?"

His eyes flashed again, so quickly she almost missed it. But she knew she'd seen it. He didn't like seeing her with Ryan.

"Andi and I are good friends," Ryan said. Heavens, the sheer volume of what people weren't saying was massive. Ryan stood close to her shoulder, and the message was clear: she wasn't alone.

She tried to dispel the tension a little bit. "Well, having a cop as a friend comes in handy sometimes." She smiled up at him, keeping her voice and expression light.

"Yeah, well, maybe you cops should be less worried

about being friends and more concerned with finding who killed my daughter." He stared at Andi. "Or have you forgotten?"

The smile slid from her face. "Oh, I haven't forgotten. Not for one single second. I'm looking forward to whoever did it being behind bars."

Silence fell for a few uncomfortable seconds.

"I guess I should get going, since you clearly have this covered." Jim shoved his hands in his pockets.

"Thanks for your concern," Andi replied, a note of dismissal in her voice. The divorce had not been an amicable one, but now that the pain of her marriage being over was gone, she realized she was holding on to bitterness. She didn't like that about herself. When had she become this person who held grudges instead of gratitude?

He went on his way and Andi let out a long, slow breath. Together, she and Ryan watched as he crossed the parking lot to his black sedan and got inside.

"You all right?" Ryan asked. He was standing close to her, so the softly spoken words tickled her ear.

She nodded. "I am. I wasn't sure if you showing up just then was a good thing or a bad thing. But I'm glad you're here, regardless."

"Me, too." He stepped away from her then, and she found she missed the closeness. She really was starting to be smitten with him and wasn't sure how to feel about it. What if he didn't feel the same? She definitely didn't want to make a fool of herself. Besides, she wasn't stupid. The situation was stressful. It wasn't the right time to be thinking about…well, romance.

He looked at the tires again. "You're going to have to get a tow to the garage. I can call who we use, if you like."

She nodded. "I'd appreciate that. I really can't be without a vehicle for long." Suddenly she realized she hadn't gone into the clinic and her lunch break was over. "Shoot. I have to tell Dr. Gonzales what's going on." She sighed. "I hate that this is affecting work."

"That's probably part of his or her goal," Ryan said. "Making you afraid, disrupting your life, having you always looking over your shoulder. The best thing is to go about your life as normally as possible." He lifted his chin toward the clinic. "Do you think you can focus enough to get through your afternoon? I can take care of the tow. I'm going to head into the office and talk to Ben about the latest, and then maybe come back and check with any businesses that have security cameras. We might be able to find something."

She hadn't thought of that. "Oh, good idea."

He touched her elbow. "At some point, they're going to make a mistake."

"I sure hope you're right."

"It's going to be okay, Andi." He reached down and took her hand, squeezed her fingers lightly. "I promise."

He let go, and she had the fleeting thought that Ryan shouldn't make promises he couldn't keep. But he was here, and he was trying. The security cameras were something she hadn't considered. She trusted Ryan to do his job.

"I should get going."

"What time are you finished? I'll come back and

take you home. I doubt your car will be ready until to-morrow morning."

She hadn't thought of that. "The clinic closes at five, and I'm usually out by five fifteen or so. I appreciate that, Ryan." She smiled, feeling suddenly shy. "You've really been going above and beyond. I don't know how to thank you."

His gaze locked with hers. "You should know by now that you don't need to thank me. I'm happy to help. I want to," he added.

"Well, thanks." Heat crept up her cheeks and she knew she needed to get back to work and stop stealing moments with him. "I'll see you in a couple of hours."

"You got it."

She went back to the clinic and turned at the door to watch him. He was standing by her car, phone to his ear, probably talking to the towing company. What had she done to deserve such a friend? She didn't know, but he was the answer to a prayer. If she were praying these days.

Maybe that was something she needed to start doing again. But would God listen?

Chapter Nine

Ryan spent the afternoon utterly frustrated.

While Sergeant Rogers agreed that the incidents were serious, there wasn't a whole lot they could do. Nothing had really escalated in the past few weeks in terms of severity, though the harassment was becoming more frequent. Hearing that this person bore a grudge but so far hadn't been threatening personal harm made Ryan grit his teeth. He knew Ben was right, but he also didn't want anything to happen to Andi. This wasn't simple mischief; there was malicious intent behind all of it. He was really starting to worry about her safety. Today it was slashing tires. Tomorrow it could be her and not the car.

Ben looked at him for a few long seconds. "Ryan, I know she's your friend. I know that your sister is her best friend. Is there a chance that…? I mean, your family is close to her. Is there a chance she's had some sort of a breakdown? It would be understandable. The anniversary of her daughter's death just passed."

"You think she's making it up?" he asked.

"I'm just trying to look at all scenarios. And I wonder if you're getting too close to be objective."

Ben was right, and Ryan took a deep breath. "No, sir," he said confidently. "I'm positive she hasn't had any sort of a breakdown. She's remarkably strong, actually. I haven't seen anything that supports that theory."

Ben nodded. "Look, I hate this as much as you do. When her daughter died, my oldest was around the same age." Ben had become a father later in his life and had told Ryan more than once what a blessing his wife and kids had turned out to be. "It's not something you forget."

"No, sir, it isn't."

"Especially for a rookie new on the scene."

Ryan swallowed tightly.

Ben sighed. "She's doing okay otherwise?" He ran his hand over his silver-gray hair. "I wish we had more to go on. The patient we talked to—Fletcher? She doesn't have an alibi for a few of the blocks of time we're looking at. I don't like her for this, though. She might have threatened Andi back then, but it looks as though she has her life together now. Mostly, anyway."

Still, it was something. "Maybe we need to follow up again. Especially since there have been developments since you spoke to her." He hesitated for a moment, then said what was on his mind. "I started looking into the babysitter again, too. Leslie. She was young, but we never really investigated. It's a loose end I'd like to tie up just in case."

Ben nodded. "Any idea of her whereabouts?"

"She'd gone to Calgary to school, but she's been back in Cadence Creek since May. The morning of the disappearance, she said she was asleep at home, it being her day off, and her parents had gone to work. It's not much, but…"

"It's worth examining. In the meantime, I can send someone to canvass the businesses around the clinic to see if they saw anything or have any camera footage."

"I'll go."

"You're off duty."

Ryan had the grace to shift uncomfortably. "I know. But I'm going back to pick Andi up from work anyway. Since she's without a car right now."

Ben's gaze held his, concern in the blue depths. "Be careful, Ryan. It's easy to get sucked into a case like this."

And a woman like this. Ryan knew what Ben was really saying, and he both appreciated and chafed against it. "Believe me, I know," Ryan admitted. "The families involved come away with a lot of baggage. It's a lot to take on. Since I think that's what you're really saying, Ben."

The older man nodded and put a hand on Ryan's shoulder. "If this crosses a line, you won't be able to work the case. There will be…consequences, professionally. You know that, so judge accordingly."

Ryan knew exactly what he meant. Just as well everything was platonic, then. "We're safe there, sir."

"Good. Let me know what you find out."

Ryan nodded and headed back out to his truck. The conversation had been fine and probably necessary, but it still left him cranky. He was worried about Andi and her safety, and he was fighting his own feelings. It would be easy to fall for her. She was kind and strong, and she made him laugh. Not to mention the way her dark hair fell over her shoulders and the warmth of her smile. Jim had been a fool to walk away from her.

He drove back to the clinic and parked where Andi had been parked and then surveyed the businesses and parking lot around him. There'd be security cameras at the bank machine, he realized, and possibly at the little electronics store since they carried games and consoles. He wasn't sure any of the cameras would extend out this far to pick up movement at the edge of the parking lot, which worked to his disadvantage. He spent over an hour talking to each business and had come up with nothing in those conversations. The business owners with cameras were all eager to be cooperative, though, so there'd be footage to go through.

At five, he was back at his truck, waiting for Andi to finish work. His stomach growled; he'd missed lunch, he realized, as he'd been at her place supervising the locksmith, and then she'd called him about her car. He could really use some dinner and downtime. His day off had ended up being busier than he intended.

Andi came out, huddled in her jacket against the October chill. He hopped out of his truck and went around the hood to open her door, smiling at her when she approached. "Your chariot awaits, madam," he joked, holding it open with a flourish.

She laughed a little. "Thank you," she said, hopping in the passenger side. He shut the door, then hopped in and started the engine. Andi leaned back in the seat, closed her eyes and sighed, and he hesitated, one hand on the wheel. She looked exhausted.

"Are you hungry?" he asked. "I missed lunch, and I'm starving."

She opened her eyes and glanced over at him. "I didn't eat, either. I was leaving for lunch when I discovered the flats. My tummy's been rumbling for the last hour and a half."

"How does the Wagon Wheel sound?"

"Like heaven."

He laughed and put the truck in gear. It only took a few minutes for them to make their way down Main Street to the diner, and Ryan parked right in front of the big windows facing the street. Andi didn't wait for him to open the door; she jumped out and slung her purse over her shoulder. "Dinner's on me," she said, as they made their way to the door.

"You don't have to do that."

"I want to. You did a ton of stuff for me today, and I'd like to repay you for that, Ryan. That's my condition for dinner."

"Then I accept."

She smiled brightly, her eyes lighting up, as if he'd given her a gift. It made him wonder again about past dynamics in her marriage. He had his pride, sure, but so did she. She was allowed to. But he wondered if that had always been the case. The more she spoke of Jim, the more he thought their marriage hadn't really been a meeting of equals. It seemed to be more Jim having things his way and Andi accommodating.

But then, who was he to judge? He had to admit that his growing feelings for her were contributing to some bias against her ex-husband, and he had to be very careful of that.

The Wagon Wheel wasn't busy; it was a Monday night and there was a smattering of people at various tables, but the atmosphere was relaxed, just what they needed. They grabbed a table, and then a waitress came over with a tiny notepad and a big smile. She couldn't be more than sixteen or seventeen, Ryan realized, with a full mouth of braces and a Cadence Creek High T-shirt paired with jeans.

She left them with menus and tall glasses of water, and moments later came back to take their orders. Ryan really was hungry, so he ordered the Monday Special of a hot beef dinner with mashed potatoes and gravy, and Andi opted for the homemade mac and cheese with garlic toast and a cup of tea. They handed back their menus. Sitting across from each other, it felt more and more like a date.

Those feelings were squashed, however, when Andi opened the conversation with the case of her slashed tires.

"You didn't have any problems with the tow company, did you?" She took the paper strip off her cutlery and napkin bundle, then fiddled with it.

"Nope. You should be able to pick it up tomorrow, complete with a new set of tires." He took a sip of his water. "Joe said he'd put on something good but not too pricey, and you can square up with him whenever." It was one of the good things about living in a small town like Cadence Creek. Quite often, neighbors looked after each other.

Ryan knew finances had been a worry when Andi's face relaxed, the tired lines softening a bit. "Oh, that's wonderful. Thank you."

"I canvassed the businesses around, too. No one remembered anything, but we've got consent to check out some cam footage."

"Do you think you'll find anything?"

She sounded so hopeful that he hated to burst her bubble. And yet he had to be honest. "I don't know, Andi. Where you parked might be out of range. I won't know until we have a look."

She frowned. "We park there so patients can have the spaces closest to the building."

"I know." He hated disappointing her. "I get that you're frustrated. We're doing the best we can."

She nodded, looking down at her place mat. "I know you are."

"Andi?"

She looked up and tears shimmered at the corners of her eyes. "Sorry. I'm just really tired."

"Of course you are. Maybe you should take a few days off work. Give yourself a chance to rest."

She shook her head, sniffed and blinked away the tears. "And what, be intimidated into not doing my job? That's not my style. Besides, then I'm just going to sit home and worry and wallow." She tried a weak smile. "I just don't understand who does something like this." She sipped at her water and her brows pulled together. "The thing I've been thinking is this. If, for example,

I had done something this awful seven years ago and got away with it, why would I suddenly draw attention back to it again and risk getting caught?"

It was a good question, and one Ryan had been thinking about, as well. "Well, the short answer is, it's someone who doesn't think they'll be caught."

"That's a tad overconfident."

"There are a few personality types that fit the bill." He folded his hands on the table. "But I'd say this person feels smarter than everyone else. Heck, even the cops are dumb. They didn't crack the case the first time."

"I wouldn't say that," she answered, her voice low. "I was upset before about there never being an arrest. But I know it wasn't because you didn't try."

"You have every right to be upset about it. Justice hasn't been served."

"Honestly?" She looked up at him with sad eyes. "It's like a book with no ending. Those final chapters are missing, where the bad guy gets what's coming to him and everyone can go on with their lives. Start to really heal. I feel so stuck. I can get so far with the process, but then I hit a wall. Because there's no…" Her voice trailed off, and he realized she was on the verge of tears.

"No closure," he said softly. "I understand."

They were quiet for a few moments as Ryan let Andi regain her composure. When she was ready, she dabbed her eyes with her napkin and lifted her head. "Okay. So back to being proactive again. Like you said before, at some point this person is going to make a mistake."

Ryan knew she was right.

He also hoped that the mistake didn't come at her expense. Because there was no way he could let anything happen to her.

Andi was mortified that she'd nearly cried in front of Ryan. She'd been honest, though, and it had been good to talk, to get some of her feelings out instead of having them churning inside her. She was also exhausted. Today's encounter with Jim had only left her more unsettled.

"Andi, are you really doing okay? I'm worried about you. I know you're not sleeping well."

"Seeing Jim was really hard today," she admitted. Her tea had arrived, and she curled her hands around the steaming cup.

Ryan sat forward. "He didn't threaten you, did he?"

She shook her head. "No, nothing like that. But after what you said the other day and thinking about our marriage..." She sighed. "I just can't wrap my head around the possibility that he could be responsible for any of this. And yet when I look back, we had problems. Ones I couldn't see, and ones I couldn't admit."

It took a lot for her to say that. She'd worked so hard to have a strong marriage. And yet it had seemed like she always fell short.

"Shelby always said Jim didn't appreciate you," Ryan said gently. "Did he hurt you, Andi?"

She shook her head, heat rising to her cheeks. "No. I mean, never with his hands. With his words. I don't think I realized how much. I...I excused a lot of it."

He nodded. She was glad he didn't ask for details.

Enumerating all her faults and shortfalls was not something she wanted to do. "And today, he just happened to be at the dollar store when I discovered my tires were slashed. It felt... I don't know. A little too coincidental."

"I know."

The waitress arrived with their plates, and Andi inhaled deeply of the delicious aromas. "Thank you," she murmured, as the waitress smiled and left them to eat.

But before she stuck her fork in the macaroni, she looked at Ryan. "I was thinking this afternoon, though. One thing stuck with me. Jim made a bit of a pointed remark about going home alone, but I'm certain he's been living with someone. Has been for a while. So why would he say that, about going home to an empty house?"

Ryan tapped his bottom lip. "That's a good point. When we visited him to tell him about reopening the case, he did say something about living alone. I hadn't heard anything about him living with someone, though there were a few decorating choices I thought seemed odd for a guy like Jim. He doesn't strike me as the type to be into flowery curtains."

"Definitely not. We never had anything with a floral pattern in the house. He hated it."

"And he didn't have anything from the dollar store. I asked if he'd been in and the clerk said yes, but that he hadn't bought or asked for anything. Just wandered around for nearly an hour, browsing."

Dread settled in the pit of her stomach. "He would have had time to do it. And he was waiting around." She could barely believe what she was saying.

Ryan cut into his slab of roast beef and shrugged. "We don't know that. But it would seem that he definitely had the opportunity."

She tried a forkful of macaroni, but it got stuck in her throat. She swallowed a few times, feeling miserable. Finally she looked up at Ryan. "He was my husband. He was her father. I don't want to believe he's capable of this."

"I know," Ryan replied softly. "Listen, we still have a few other leads we're following up on. I'm not going to make any assumptions without solid proof, okay? To do that might mean missing something else. Something that would keep you safe."

"I feel safe when I'm with you," she said, and meant it.

His cheeks colored a bit as he stabbed his fork into a slice of bright orange carrot. "I'm glad." His voice was low, and the timbre of it rode along her nerve endings. She hadn't felt this way in so long. Maybe it was because she was so tired or that Ryan always seemed to come to her rescue. She was vulnerable.

She scooped up a forkful of mac and cheese and shoveled it in her mouth. She should not be attracted to a man because she needed rescuing! There was a good chance these feelings weren't even real. She'd be better off spending her time trying to figure out who was behind everything that had been happening.

To her relief, Ryan changed the subject to Shelby's family and Carson's latest antics, which dissolved the tension that had arisen between them. Before long, he had her laughing, and she realized with a start that she'd eaten every last bit of her dinner. It was the first time she'd been able to finish a meal in nearly two weeks. Maybe she didn't need rescuing, but she was glad for the distraction.

When the waitress came back, she asked for more tea, and they both ordered pie. They were just waiting when Andi heard her name from a familiar voice. "Mrs. Wallace?"

She turned in the booth and saw Leslie Kenney approaching, her pretty blue eyes wide with surprise and a smile on her lips. "Les?"

"It's me! Oh, it's good to see you."

Andi slid out of the booth and greeted her old babysitter with a warm hug. "You look wonderful, Leslie. All grown up."

"I graduated university in May. But I haven't found a job yet, so I'm living with my parents for now. It's not great."

"I suppose not." Leslie had to be in her late twenties now. "The market's tough, though."

"It's good to see you," Leslie said. She slid her gaze to Ryan, and Andi saw the speculative gleam in her eye. "I don't want to interrupt your date."

"Oh, it's not a… Well, anyway, do you remember Ryan Davenport? Shelby's brother?"

"Oh, right! I knew you looked familiar. Nice to see you again."

"Likewise," he said, but Andi thought she detected a coolness in his voice. She didn't know why. Leslie had always been lovely.

"We should get together for coffee or something soon

and catch up on everything," Andi suggested, giving Leslie another squeeze.

"I'd like that. A lot. I'll see you later."

She left, and Andi sat back down in the booth. "Wow, that was a surprise. And not as hard as I would have thought. She looks great."

"When did you see her last?"

"Honestly? Chelsea's funeral. I did reach out once, but she said she wasn't ready to talk to me. I couldn't judge her for that. Everyone deals with things differently."

The pie came and the subject was dropped. Andi started laughing at the expression on Ryan's face. The meringue on his lemon pie stood a good four inches in height, perfectly white and fluffy with delicate browning on the top. Her slice was apple, topped with vanilla bean ice cream. It was huge, but she was determined. The pie here was one of the best things.

Finally, her tummy stuffed to the limit, she sat back in her chair and let out a sigh. "My goodness. As Shelby would say, I have a food baby." She patted her stomach and laughed. "I haven't eaten that much in months."

"I think that's a good thing." Ryan pushed his plate away. "Especially if you've found it difficult to eat."

"It's just the anxiety," she replied. "I'm fine. This will get resolved." She met his gaze. "We'll find who's doing this and who killed Chelsea. And when that's over, I'm going to sleep for a week. Maybe a year."

"I'm so sorry," Ryan said, reaching over and touching her hand. "I wish this was over for you now."

She squeezed his fingers, then drew her hand back,

remembering her resolve to not be needy. "Me, too. But it's not. I know you're working on it. I'm not angry at you or the investigation. This guy doesn't want to be caught. He's having too much fun playing the game."

As soon as she said it, she realized how true it was. "That's it, Ryan. It's not just that they don't think they'll be caught. This is a game and they're having fun with it. So maybe we need to come up with a way to not play along."

She wasn't quite sure how to do that, but the idea filled her with a new purpose and resolve. "I'm done being the victim here," she said, her voice firm and steady. "I'm done playing one. And when whoever this is figures that out? That's when they'll slip up, and we'll have them."

Ryan's troubled gaze met hers. "Be careful, Andi. There's a fine line between not being a victim and pro-voking someone. The goal here is to keep you safe. Not for you to get hurt."

He was only partly right. "The goal is to arrest this person. And keep me safe at the same time. Don't worry. I won't take any unnecessary chances."

Chapter Ten

It was dark by the time they finished their meal and went back outside to Ryan's truck. They stopped a moment to talk to Tyson and Clara Diamond, who were just leaving the nearby bakery and café. Andi had always liked Clara. She ran the women's shelter in town, and she and Ty were such a cute couple. When Chelsea had gone missing, Clara and her sister-in-law Angela had been among the first to offer their support.

Andi also saw Clara's gaze flicker between Andi and Ryan, surreptitiously assessing. If Andi were being honest with herself, she liked being treated as part of a couple, even if it wasn't real. What might it be like if all this had never happened, and Ryan had asked her out on a date?

"You should both come to the pre-Thanksgiving get-together we're having at the ranch on Thursday," Clara suggested, digging slightly.

Ryan's gaze landed on Andi and she sensed his discomfort. "Oh, us?" She kept her voice light. "We're not a thing, Clara. Just friends. Ryan helped me out of a tight spot earlier today and I paid him back with supper."

Clara's cheeks pinkened. "Oh, I'm sorry." Ty nudged her arm and she sighed. "I know. I need to stop sticking my nose in."

Andi couldn't help but laugh. "It's perfectly okay, isn't it, Ryan?"

"No worries at all," he said, but the question had caused another one of those awkward vibes between them. After tonight, she couldn't be calling him for every little thing. She was certain that while she was developing feelings for him, he didn't feel the same. Instead, it felt as if lines were being blurred. She'd taken advantage of his friendship.

"Well, we should be going. We only have a sitter until eight thirty, since it's a school night." Clara provided a graceful exit, and within moments they'd said their goodbyes and Ryan was once again holding the truck door open for her.

"All set?" he asked, starting the engine.

"I am. It was a nice time, especially seeing Leslie. Though I'm so full you could just give me a nudge and I could roll home."

He laughed. "Naw. It's a short drive. Which reminds me." He dug into his jacket pocket and took out two keys. "Keys for your new locks."

She took them from his fingers and dug in her purse for her key chain... Then realized her keys were with her car at the garage. She dropped them in her purse instead. "Thanks again for doing all that."

"I don't mind." He pulled out of the parking spot and headed down the street, then turned right at the stop sign. She lived within the town limits, but a little closer to the edge, where the lots were slightly bigger with more privacy. These days she kind of wished she didn't have so much privacy. Otherwise, a neighbor might have seen something.

Ryan kept glancing in his rearview mirror, his lips in a set line.

"Something wrong?"

"What? Oh, no. Just thinking out my plan for tomorrow."

But his gaze kept shifting to the mirror. When they turned down her street, his facial expression eased. A vehicle passed behind them a few seconds later. "Did you think we were being followed?"

He turned his head to look at her. "What makes you say that?"

"I don't know—checking the mirror every five seconds?" She raised an eyebrow.

"I'm just vigilant," he remarked. His lips were relaxed now, not drawn so tightly. But she wasn't convinced. Suddenly the thought of spending the night alone in her house wasn't so comfortable. *You're not going to be a victim*, she reminded herself. *You can do this. You have to do this.*

He drove into her yard and put the truck in Park. Once again, her porch light was off, since she'd expected to be home shortly after five. She got her keys, and he left his headlights on but got out and walked her to the door. "I'm just going to do a quick check of the house. Indulge me. It'll make me feel better."

She opened the door and let him in, flicking on lights as she stepped over the threshold. She waited in the tiny foyer while he went inside and checked out all the rooms, then clomped down into the basement. "Everything looks okay. Do you want to look around and see if anything is out of place?"

She went through the house, room by room, but didn't notice anything out of the ordinary. "I think it's okay," she answered, going back to the kitchen. "I don't see anything where it shouldn't be."

"Good. I'll check outside."

She hung her purse on the hook and waited. This was her life now. Coming home and checking to see if someone had invaded her private space. If someone was trying to hurt her. Ryan came back a few minutes later, his face tight again. "What happened?"

"I think someone was fooling with one of your basement windows," he said.

This came as a relief. "Actually, they won't have much luck there. After Jim left, I had the basement windows nailed shut. The only way anyone is getting in is to actually break them. I always lock my doors, you know? I mean, everyone says Cadence Creek is safe, but look what happened to Chelsea."

She admitted something she'd never said to anyone before. "To be honest, Ryan, I haven't truly felt safe since the day she was taken. I deal with it better, and I try to use logic, but I do take normal precautions."

She bit down on her lip. "That's why discovering

that photo was so hard. I lock my doors. It didn't keep them out." She still didn't mention Jim. After all, they only had a hunch and a bunch of coincidences, but no actual proof tying him to anything. She wasn't going to treat his guilt as a foregone conclusion.

"We already established that Jim could have had a key," he reminded her. "With no sign of forced entry—"

"That still doesn't prove anything. Look, Jim and I are divorced, and it wasn't very amicable. That doesn't mean he's guilty of this." She frowned. She kept going back and forth about it. Was it denial? Or were they focusing on Jim because it was easy to paint an ex as a villain? Sometimes she'd come close to believing it, and then she simply couldn't. They'd been married for six years. Parents together for three. Jim had been a jerk, but he'd never been violent.

"Why do you constantly defend him?" Ryan's tone sharpened.

His tone surprised her. Was he angry with her? For giving someone the benefit of the doubt? "Why are you so determined to vilify him?" she shot back.

His mouth settled in a thin line. "I'm not. I just think—"

"You don't like him. I get it." She interrupted him again, frustration finally bubbling over, breaking the spell that had surrounded them over dinner. "If it's any consolation, I don't like him much, either. But it's a long way from there to what you're accusing him of."

Ryan shoved his hands in his pockets as they stared at each other. "Maybe I don't like him on principle. Because he left you. Because he didn't appreciate what he had. And because I'm sure he never treated you as well as you deserved."

Well, that was a mouthful for him to say, wasn't it? Andi wasn't sure how to feel about it. There were times she'd thought exactly the same things, but hearing Ryan voice them was different. "I think that's probably for me to say, though, isn't it?"

His face flattened. "Look, is it so wrong that I'm worried about your safety?"

Andi tried not to let her emotions take over. She wasn't sure what she felt, if she were honest. On one hand, she loved knowing Ryan cared. She didn't trust her own feelings, though, or her judgment. She still wondered if her attraction to him was based on the heightened emotions of the situation. She was all over the map.

"It's not wrong," she said, her voice softer. "And I appreciate it more than you know."

"I don't want your appreciation." His brows were knitted together, and she could tell by the snap in his voice he wasn't appeased. Her annoyance flared again.

"Then what do you want, Ryan?"

He didn't answer. They stared at each other while the air between them got heavier with unsaid words. Andi's patience was wearing to a thread. She'd already been vulnerable on the anniversary of Chelsea's death, but the events of the past few weeks had worn her down. She wasn't sleeping, wasn't eating regularly. She was in a constant state of anxiety. She was just tired enough to be frustrated that he was fixated on Jim but the police seemed no closer to catching the culprit.

She really was relying on him too much. Maybe she should stop thinking that and start doing something about it.

"Look," she said, taking another step back. "I appreciate everything you've done, but this is… I mean, I can't call you for every little thing. It's not fair to you. If anything more happens, I'll call the detachment." That probably sounded cold, but she wasn't capable of more.

"Andi, I didn't mean to cross a line…"

"I know." She sighed. "And neither did I. But I did on that first day when I called you instead of calling the detachment. I took advantage of a family friendship, and I've been taking advantage of it ever since."

Why did he suddenly look hurt?

"I've never minded. You should know that. I care about you, Andi. Not just because you're Shelby's best friend. But because you're you."

Having someone say they care should be a lovely, heartwarming moment. Instead, it just added another layer onto her stress. "I don't know what to do with that right now," she admitted. "There's just too much happening. And I think us getting closer has… Well, I don't want to say compromised your judgment, but I think you dislike Jim on a personal level that has nothing to do with evidence. That's not good, Ryan. You told me that first day that you must approach a crime scene and let it give you the answers without imposing any sort of agenda on it. What kind of evidence do you have to point to Jim? Other than the fact that he's not a particularly nice guy and he had the opportunity?"

Ryan closed his eyes briefly. "You're right. I know

you're right. I can't tell what's intuition and what's bias right now."

"I know you want to protect me, and I appreciate that. But I think you need to step back for a bit. From this case and from me."

It actually pained her to say it, even though she knew it was the right thing. His feelings weren't the only ones mixed up.

He nodded. "Okay. Okay. But promise me that you'll call the detachment if anything happens and 911 if you're in immediate danger. Do you hear me?" He came forward and put his strong hands on her upper arms. She looked up and wondered for a moment what it would be like to kiss him. She swallowed thickly, overwhelmed by the thought and knowing it would be a huge mistake to follow that inclination.

"I promise. I want to stay safe, too, you know." She tried a smile instead.

He nodded, the motion curt. "All right. In that case, I'd better get going."

Ryan went to the door and lifted his hand in a wave as he went out and shut the door behind him.

"Dear Lord, please tell me I just did the right thing," she said to the empty kitchen.

Thirty seconds later he was back, giving a short knock and sticking his head in the door, looking sheepish.

"I left my lights on when we got here, and it drained my battery. Can you give me a boost?"

She couldn't help it; she started to chuckle, and then the chuckle went to a full-on laugh, and before they knew it, the two of them were cracking up, gasping for breath and wiping their eyes.

"Oh, I think I needed that," she said, still gasping and chuckling.

"Me, too," he admitted. "I'm sorry about earlier."

"Don't be. I think we probably needed to clear the air a bit. And I'm sorry I seem all over the place." The honesty of their discussion and the laughter had gone a long way toward relieving some of the tension she'd been feeling.

"Friends?"

Her heart softened. "Of course we are. I have a battery charger in the garage. Hang on."

It took them a few minutes to get out the charger and then hook it up to his truck, but before long, his engine was revving and there was no reason left for him to hang around. Andi rolled up the cables and stowed the charger back in the garage, locking the garage door before stepping into the swath of his headlights.

"Thanks," he said, "for the rescue. Now I'm going to owe you dinner."

As much as she wanted to say yes, she knew she couldn't. Instead, she prevaricated with a "Maybe when all this is over."

"Fair enough." His face sobered again. "Please be careful, Andi."

"I will. I promise."

His gaze dropped to her lips and then back up to her eyes again, and she knew he'd meant it when he said he cared about her. But he stepped away and around the open door of his truck, then hopped into the cab. The slam of his door echoed through the fall evening.

She headed to the house, knowing he'd want her safely inside before driving away. At the threshold, she lifted a hand to wave at him but didn't look to see if he waved back before backing out of her driveway. Instead, she shut the door and locked it.

Once his taillights disappeared, she sank down on the sofa, in the dark, and sighed. She knew she had to take care of herself. And yet she couldn't bring herself to go to her bedroom and crawl under the covers. She hadn't slept in her bed for three days now—the last two at home she'd slept here, on the sofa, and last night, which seemed like forever ago, she'd been at Shelby's.

She put her phone on the table next to her, grabbed a blanket and made herself as comfortable as possible. Tomorrow was another workday, and there was no way she'd give this person the satisfaction of deviating from her normal schedule. She just hoped something came up soon, because this wasn't a lifestyle she could maintain indefinitely.

And she suspected that whoever was stalking her knew that.

Ryan hated driving away from Andi's house. Too many things were happening, and deep down he had reservations about her staying there alone. It made her far too vulnerable. But what could he do?

The radio played quietly in the otherwise silent cab, but it was plenty noisy inside his head. He kept going over everything Andi had said tonight, about his fixation with Jim, about evidence, about all of it. She'd been totally right, so why couldn't he flip his brain to be on board? He knew he had to let the evidence do the talking, but his gut was telling him something different. Was she right? Was it because he didn't like Jim? Was it because—and this one stopped him up—he was jealous? Protective? Territorial?

He dismissed the last one. Territorial was possessiveness, and he wasn't okay with that. A woman wasn't something to be owned. She was her own person, entitled to respect and love.

Love.

He looked both ways at a stop sign before easing forward carefully. *Okay, let's put a pin in that.* He had to go back to what she said earlier tonight during their argument. Or as she put it, clearing the air. She was right—what they needed was proof. Actual evidence that led somewhere.

They'd missed something. He just knew it. The encounter with Leslie only muddied the waters. On the surface she seemed lovely and friendly. The affection she'd shown Andi hadn't seemed forced. Right now she fit three criteria: she'd had the opportunity, she'd been close to the family, and she'd been in Cadence Creek both at the time of the murder and now.

Not a lot to go on.

For several minutes, Ryan went through details in his head. He sifted through the fine points of each incident as he reached home, went inside, got a glass of water and got ready for bed. It wasn't until he was lying in his bed, hands behind his head and staring at the ceiling, that he spoke out loud.

"Okay, God. What am I supposed to do now? What am I missing?"

There was no ready answer, and Ryan let out a huff. But what had he been expecting? For the skies to open up and a booming voice to come down and give him instruction? He knew that wasn't really how prayer worked. So he waited, letting out a breath, releasing all the questions and demands, and simply thinking, *What now, Lord?*

In the quiet, the answer came. It was simple and true, and it gave Ryan's heart some peace as he absorbed it.

Protect her.

It was his job to protect her. His inclinations had been correct, but he hadn't been going about it the right way, had he? The best way to protect her wasn't just answering her calls and doing favors. It was finding out who was behind the harassment. Starting tomorrow morning, he was going over everything with a fine-tooth comb.

If she didn't want him around all the time, that was fine. He had to focus now. It was his job. And his sacred duty.

Chapter Eleven

Andi rose earlier than normal, packed her lunch and set out on the walk to work. It was a couple of miles into the town center where the clinic was, and the fall day was crisp and cool. After work she'd head over to the garage to pick up her car and put a little money toward her bill. Hopefully next payday she could pay off the rest.

All along the walk she made sure to be aware of her surroundings. It was 8:00 a.m., so there was some traffic, mostly heading out of town for the commute into Red Deer or some even as far as Calgary, though those commuters tended to leave much earlier. Local traffic was a lazier, more relaxed pace, just like the town. The leaves were mostly gone from the trees now, the bare branches clacking together in the northern breeze. Still, the sky was clear, and when she looked up, she saw a huge V of geese heading south. Before long, it would be winter, and she'd be scraping the frost from her windshield and checking the forecast for snow.

As she looked around her, everything seemed normal. She didn't get the sense of being followed, either, or of eyes watching her. That sensation always made her shiver.

Once at work, she tried to put everything behind her and just focus on her job. There were some well-baby appointments, and this time of year was always busier with flu shot appointments and vaccines. Dr. Gonzales asked if she was doing better today, and she smiled and replied yes, appreciating the care and concern.

But just after ten thirty, the receptionist, Emily, came back into the exam room area with a frown on her face and a concerned look in her eyes.

"Andi? There's someone in the waiting room who wants to see you. She doesn't have an appointment, though, and when I said we could book her in next week, she got quite agitated and said she needs to see you now. She's refusing to leave."

Andi's pulse leaped. It was an unusual request at a really turbulent time, and frankly, it made her nervous.

"Did she give her name?"

"No. She said you'd know her when you saw her."

Andi didn't want Emily to bear the brunt of any unpleasantness. "I'll come out, but if anything goes sideways, call the police, okay?"

Emily gave a few quick nods. She was only in her early twenties, sweet, but she hadn't had to deal with difficult patients much yet. Andi took a few seconds to gather herself together. This was a public space. There were people in the waiting room. She would be fine.

Her work shoes made soft sounds on the floor as she

followed Emily to the waiting area. As soon as she saw who was waiting, she knew what it was about. Roxanne Fletcher was waiting there, her hair in a ponytail, wearing faded jeans and a sweater. She was neat and tidy but clearly anxious. "Ms. Wallace," she said, her voice filled with relief. "Thank you. Can we talk somewhere?"

Andi was still nervous. After all, the RCMP had questioned her about Chelsea and the latest incidents. "We have patients waiting, Mrs. Fletcher. Perhaps we could schedule an appointment."

"You do remember me. I half hoped you wouldn't."

Andi's stomach twisted. "Yes, I remember you," she said carefully.

"I just want to talk to you. About what happened. The police came to see me…"

"I'm not sure that's a good idea, Roxanne." She kept her voice as even as she could, even though her heart was galloping a mile a minute. Roxanne was clearly nervous, but Andi couldn't tell the reason or get a read on the other woman's state of mind.

The waiting room was a rapt audience, and Andi was torn between being grateful for their presence and wishing this conversation was happening in private. Heads turned to whomever was speaking, taking it all in. Cadence Creek was small. This exchange would be all over town in a matter of hours.

"Please," Roxanne pleaded. "I just want to apologize. In private." The woman's blue eyes welled with tears.

"Everything okay out here?"

Dr. Gonzales joined Andi, who was suddenly grateful for the support. "A former patient who wants to speak with me privately," she said quietly.

"Is it safe?" Dr. Gonzales spoke right by Andi's ear.

"I hope so," she whispered.

Dr. Gonzales stepped forward. "Ms...."

"Fletcher. Roxanne Fletcher."

"Come with me," Dr. Gonzales instructed.

"Oh, but I wanted to speak to the nurse. To Ms. Wallace."

"This is your only chance to speak at all, without an appointment. Are you coming or not?"

Roxanne followed, and Dr. Gonzales led her into an open exam room. "We're leaving the door open, Roxanne." She gestured to a chair. "You may speak to Andi here, but I'll be across the hall in my office. You understand what we're saying?"

Roxanne nodded quickly. "Yes. And thank you."

The door was left open as Andi went in and sat on the rolling stool usually used by the doctor. "All right, Roxanne. You have my attention. What did you come here to say?"

Now that the moment was upon her, Roxanne fell silent. Andi waited. She was sure it had to do with the police questioning and what had happened all those years ago. She was cautious now, sitting closest to the door, knowing her boss was right across the hall and listening. But oddly enough, she didn't feel in danger. Considering how she was constantly on high alert, it was strange to realize she didn't feel threatened.

Finally Roxanne started to speak. "I need to say... that is...what happened a long time ago..." She cleared her throat, but still stared at her lap. "I'm so sorry for how I reacted that day. What I said."

Andi remained silent. She had long ago understood that letting the silence sit often led to the other person revealing more, so she was patient.

"I, uh…" Roxanne looked up, finally. As soon as she met Andi's gaze, her eyes filled with tears again. "It was so hard, getting that news. I was so angry. So overwhelmed. I took it out on you, and I said awful things. But I never meant them, Ms. Wallace. I would never wish harm on another child."

"I know the police spoke to you, Mrs. Fletcher."

Roxanne nodded. "They did. I didn't understand why, really, until I realized they were asking about your little one's murder. Oh, Ms. Wallace. I'm so awful sorry that happened. It was just tragic. I came today because ever since I talked to the police I've been up nights, thinking about what happened to you and what I said. I never apologized, and I know you might not want it now or might not care. But I want to give it anyway. I'm so sorry for what I said, and I'm sorry about your little girl." A tear rolled down her cheek and she wiped it away, but she never stopped looking at Andi's face.

Andi was having a hard time keeping control of her emotions, too. She remembered that day very well; she'd told Ryan about it, after all. "You were distraught, Roxanne. You'd just received terrible news. I never took it personally."

"I blamed you and the doctor. It wasn't your fault. I know that. I knew it then. I just didn't know what to do with all my emotions."

"I know that. It's all right."

Roxanne nodded. "I don't know what's going on now. The police asked me about all these times and where I was, and my husband's away in the oil patch and I'm usually home alone… But I swear, Ms. Wallace, whatever is going on, I never held a grudge against you and wish nothing but the best for you. I couldn't go on any longer having you think that I…" She stopped, swallowed loudly. "I could never hurt a child. Or someone who'd lost a baby. I know what that's like. I wouldn't wish that on anybody."

Andi tried valiantly to keep from crying, as well. The apology was as heartfelt as she'd ever heard. "Did you ever have any children, Mrs. Fletcher?"

Roxanne shook her head. "No. We tried, but after a few miscarriages we gave up. It was destroying me and our marriage, too."

"I'm so sorry."

"Not your fault, Ms. Wallace. And I mean that."

Andi reached over and took Roxanne's hand. Roxanne clasped it back and held it for a long time. While they were linked, Andi thought a quick prayer for peace of mind and heart for them both. It was the first time she'd prayed in a long time, and it felt as natural to her as beams of sunlight soaking into her skin on a summer day. *Oh*, she thought, realizing that, somehow, Roxanne's visit had given her back something she'd been missing for a very long time.

"I should let you get back to work now," Roxanne said. "But thank you for seeing me. For letting me apologize. It was eating me up inside. I'm not sure I'd have had the courage to come back later."

Andi knew what guilt felt like, how it gnawed away at all the best parts of you until it seemed there was nothing of value left. As they stood, she looked Roxanne dead in the eye and said, "I forgive you."

Roxanne's lip wobbled. "Thank you. And whatever is going on, I hope the end result is what you need. What you're looking for."

An arrest in the death of her daughter. Andi knew that all of the anxiety of the past few weeks would be worth it all if it somehow led to Chelsea's killer. "Me, too," she replied. "Me, too."

After work, Andi made her way to the garage. It was on the other side of town, a block and a half off Main Street, and it felt good to stretch her legs and roll her shoulders after the long day. The emotion of the morning's run-in with Roxanne had, at first, been a rush of adrenaline. But it had been followed by an energy crash around two o'clock. She was tired, but the walk helped even her out. Besides, once she got her car back, she'd drive home, make some dinner and have a good long soak in the tub.

She bit down on her lip. That was as long as something else wasn't waiting for her at home. It wasn't the least bit fun, living on tenterhooks, wondering what was right around the corner.

The car was ready, and she paid two hundred toward the bill, which was substantially larger than just tires because the tow was included. Still, she'd manage—she always did. She was fortunate to live in a town where people knew each other and would give a little grace now and then. She got inside and started the engine, then gave the dash a little pat. "Sorry 'bout that," she said to the car. "You're all better now."

Once at home, she let herself inside with the key Ryan had given her. The air was still, as if waiting for her, and she let out a slow breath. Coming home had been a refuge for so long; it was odd now to find it was a source of stress and anxiety. She locked the door behind her, then put down her purse and toed off her shoes. Tonight she was tired, but she was determined to have a normal evening. She was going to make a nice dinner for herself—maybe some pasta and salad—and then take a hot soak in the tub.

After washing her hands, she put a chicken breast in the microwave to thaw and dug out some broccoli, mushrooms and cream. Chicken, veg and pasta in a cream sauce sounded perfect. As she put water on for the pasta, she started to hum the song that had been on the car radio. Garlic and olive oil went in the pan, followed by tiny cubes of chicken breast. Her mouth was already watering when she started the cream sauce.

She dropped a blob of butter into the cream and the liquid splashed up onto her scrubs. "Oh, no," she said, frowning. She turned down the burners and headed for the bedroom to change out of her scrub shirt and into a hoodie. But when she entered her room, she screamed.

On top of her duvet were three daisies.

Andi pressed her hand to her heart, the jolts of anger and fear feeling familiar, which only made her angrier. They'd changed the locks, checked all the windows.

And yet somehow someone had been in here—again. She rushed forward and grabbed the daisies, then took them to the kitchen and threw them in the trash. She checked the door. Nothing looked jimmied or chipped from trying to force the lock. Furious, she stomped down into the basement and checked all the windows. They were still nailed firmly shut. Not a single thing was out of place. It was like the flowers had dropped out of nowhere, right on her bed, just to play with her mind.

She sank her fingers into her hair and fisted them, so done with all of it. Then she stomped upstairs, out the back door and onto the small deck. "Coward!" she shouted, not caring anymore who heard. "I'm right here, you big chicken!"

Then she felt absolutely foolish.

She went back inside and shut the door, wondering if the neighbors had heard and what they must think of all the goings-on lately. She stared at the little bench and row of hooks on the wall and the brand-new key hanging there. "Fat lot of good you did," she groused, and then went still.

Key. Not keys. There was only one on her key ring now. What in the world? There had been two last night when she'd pulled them out of her purse in Ryan's truck. Now there was one.

Had someone used the other key to get inside today? And how had they got hold of it, anyway? She slammed the lid over the pan with the chicken, turned off the burner and fumed. This person just had everything going their way, didn't they? They never left clues or made a mistake. Always knew when she wasn't home. None of the neighbors ever saw anything...

She took the key off the hook, shoved on her shoes and went out, locking the door behind her. For fifteen minutes she went door to door, asking if anyone had seen someone in her yard or a strange car around earlier in the day. Nothing. Not a single thing. This person was a ghost. Either that or they knew exactly how to access her property without anyone seeing...

She stood in her driveway and stared out over her backyard. The houses on this street backed onto a walking path that led from the high school to the side streets in what she supposed could loosely be termed "the suburbs"—more like the total residential area of Cadence Creek, away from the small nucleus of businesses. Someone could access her property without a whole lot of trouble. Granted, she had let the shrubs and little trees grow over the past few years. But it was possible.

Her shoes crunched on the gravel as she went to the top of the driveway and onto the grass leading to the trees and shrubs bordering her yard. It didn't take long, now that she was looking for something in particular. About thirty feet to the right of the garage, there was a narrow path through the brush, only as wide as a footprint, really. Weeds and seedlings had grown enough that a person could walk by and totally miss it. Andi stepped onto the tiny path and followed it carefully, noting where the grass and weeds were crushed. Her lot extended back about sixty feet through the trees, where suddenly it opened up onto the unpaved path. The town kept it maintained with crusher dust, and she looked to the right and left.

There wasn't a soul on it tonight. Not even the early evening walkers she sometimes heard.

It would be the perfect way to access her property.
Especially since there were at least two other streets
nearby. Someone could park and walk to her place in a
matter of a few minutes.

It still didn't explain the key, but it was something.

She turned and walked back to the house, keeping
her eyes peeled for anything out of the ordinary. Twelve
seconds. That was all it took to go from the path to her
backyard. Why had she not thought of this before?

She took another five steps and her head snapped
up. Her smoke alarm was going off. What in the world?

The key was stiff in the lock as she tried to open the
door. When she finally managed, smoke was billowing
through the kitchen and the smoke alarm was screaming in her ears, but she couldn't see any flames. Fan-
ning her hand in front of her face, she ran to the stove
and saw the charred bottom of the saucepan where she'd
put the cream and milk. She grabbed the plastic handle
of the saucepan and shoved it off the burner, and then
looked at the dial. Instead of turning it off, she'd turned
it up. The milk had boiled up and over, creating a huge
mess on the burner, and then the remainder had burned
on the bottom, the charred remains causing the smoke.
Andi grabbed a chair and hopped onto it so she could
disconnect the smoke alarm, then went to the sink and
opened the window, hoping the draft would suck the
smoke outside.

She was so tired of all of it.

For the next thirty minutes she cleaned up the mess,

and then she sat on her sofa and stared at her phone. She shouldn't call Ryan. She'd promised herself she wouldn't. But this was something important. Two things, really. Both the appearance of the daisies and the path through to her backyard.

She dialed his number, and it rang several times before going to voice mail. Of course, he could be on shift or out doing something. His life certainly didn't revolve around her, did it? She left a brief message saying she had some new information for him, then clicked off the phone. Did she ever. Between Roxanne paying her a visit, the flowers and the trail, it felt as if everything was speeding up.

And she didn't feel that safe, either. She called Shelby and asked if she could spend a couple of days at her place. Whoever was determined to mess with her seemed to enjoy the fact that she was alone, and they could come and go without detection. That could never happen at Shelby's busy house. There was strength in numbers.

Shelby immediately agreed when Andi filled her in. "Are you sure it's okay? I don't want to put your family in any danger."

"Don't give it another thought. You'll be safe here. Ian and I are here, and we've got a security system and a trail cam."

"You have a camera?"

Shelby laughed. "The kids like to see what wildlife wanders through. It's kind of fun. Anyway, of course you can come here. Have you told Ryan your plans?"

Heat rushed up Andi's neck. "No, of course not."

"You should. He'll want to make sure you're safe, too."

"I'll touch base with him later. Anyway, let me throw a few things in a bag and then I'll be over."

"I'll put on the kettle and we can have some tea, and I made a coffee cake today. If I can keep the nematodes that are my children out of it, it'll be our treat after they go to bed."

Andi's body began to relax. Her best friend was so good to her. "I'll be there in thirty minutes," she replied, and hung up to pack.

Chapter Twelve

R yan wiped his hands over his eyes and stared at the computer screen again. His on-duty hours had been spent on patrol and he got the feeling Ben was keeping him in a cruiser to keep him away from the case. That didn't stop him from following up on the details. Ever since Andi had called him and told him about the daisies and the path, he'd spent his spare moments poring over reports—from the current case and the one seven years ago.

Andi didn't believe Roxanne Fletcher had anything to do with what was happening, and neither did Ryan. Roxanne's husband might not be around right now, but he'd been working locally when Chelsea had gone missing, and employment records showed that Roxanne had been working at the Diamond ranch, helping Mrs. Diamond with the fall deep cleaning that whole week. Her agency's payroll records confirmed it.

A canvass of the areas near the path behind Andi's house hadn't turned up anything, but at least now if neighbors were aware, they'd be on the lookout for anything out of place. He could kick himself for not thinking of entering the property from the back. This was Andi's well-being at stake; he couldn't overlook that sort of detail again.

She'd thrown out the daisies, too. No evidence there to lead to anyone.

Frustrated, he minimized the screen and sat back in his chair. Tonight was the pre-Thanksgiving get-together at the Diamond ranch, and Shelby had told him he had to go. He didn't feel like being social, but Andi was going to be there. She had taken the evening off work and was going with Shelby and family, and he felt bad about not seeing her the past few days. Truthfully, he'd been working and following up on all the developments, including the missing second key. He'd actually gone over there last night and run a rolling magnet over her driveway to see if she'd dropped it and hadn't found it.

He needed to get out and clear his head. Quite often, the best answers came to him when he stopped looking for them. Besides, Clara, Ty, Angela and Sam put on a good time. They'd probably open up the bottom of one of the barns and have music and food.

When he arrived, dressed in jeans and a sweater to ward off the October chill, there were already a good dozen cars parked along the side of the long driveway. He saw Shelby's minivan and knew Andi was already here. He ran a hand over his hair and then caught himself, chuckling a little at worrying about his appearance. There was no denying he was quite taken with her. Maybe once this was over, he'd ask her out on an actual date.

When he arrived at the barn, the chatter was at full volume and music was a low hum below the voices. A trio of kids, one of whom was Carson, went racing by on their way to the yard behind the house, which was a veritable playground of swings, a slide and things to climb on. When he turned around again, Andi was there, about twenty feet away, looking at him. When their eyes met, it was like a punch to his gut. He'd been afraid of her baggage, or at least that was what he'd told himself. But that wasn't truly it, he realized. He wasn't afraid of taking it on. He was afraid of messing it up. Of caring for someone so incredible and then losing her. Especially since she was Shelby's best friend. Someone like Andi could break his heart, and then he'd have to see her all the time and be reminded of what he'd lost.

It still frightened him. But he'd got to know her a lot better over the past few weeks. He was almost at the place where it might be worth the risk. Getting past these current troubles and making her smile again? Seemed like a really good place to be headed.

He made his way over to her, his breath frozen in his chest.

"Hi," she said, smiling up at him. "You came."

"Clara did invite both of us," he said. When her cheeks flushed, he added, "I'm kidding, Andi. I know you came with Shelby tonight."

"I'm still…" She looked up at him from beneath her lashes. "I'm still glad you came."

"You doing all right?"

She nodded. "Shelby's so wonderful. And I feel safe. Though I can't stay there forever."

"Of course not. With the new leads from last week, I'm sure something will break soon." He wanted to talk to her about everything that had happened since Monday, but not here and not now. Tonight was supposed to be social and fun. He nodded at her paper cup. "What's in there?"

"Warm apple cider," she said, beaming. "It's delicious. And there's food, too. Some savory kinds of finger foods and a ton of baked goods. Shelby made butter tarts and they're already gone."

He groaned. Butter tarts were a favorite, and Shelby had inherited their mother's recipe.

"Don't worry." She leaned over as if sharing a secret. "Shelby saved a half dozen for you back at the house."

"I could use some of that cider," he said. Her nearness meant he could smell the vanilla scent of her hair and the light perfume she wore. She looked so cute tonight, too, in jeans and cowboy boots and a long chocolate-brown sweater. She looked like an ad for autumn.

He got some cider, and then he and Andi separated for a while to mingle with the other guests. He caught up with Callum Shepard, who had a dairy farm just outside of town, and both Diamond brothers. It wasn't until he spoke to Angela Diamond, though, that the evening took on a different tone.

They were standing to one side, chatting about the ranch, when Angela said, "Clara mentioned that you and Andi were at the Wagon Wheel the other night."

She smiled up at him. "I'm not trying to pry, but curious minds…"

He laughed. "So you're going to pry anyway? Not much to tell, Angela. I'd helped her out of a jam, and she paid me back with dinner. It was no big deal."

"Well, you're a step up from her ex, anyway." Angela scowled and turned her cup of cider around in her hands. "Jim was really no prize."

"She really doesn't talk about him much," Ryan replied.

"Not much wonder. She's been through a lot. He's here occasionally, you know. We get our equipment from his dealer, and he's sold us a few pieces over the years. Sam says he's okay." The look on her face said otherwise.

"What makes you say he was no prize?"

She took a sip of cider. "I shouldn't say anything."

Ryan faced her and made eye contact. "I'd like to know, Angela." He didn't want to say anything about Andi's troubles, but a little insight into her ex-husband could be a huge help.

"Off the record?" she asked. When he nodded, she let out a sigh. "He just rubs me the wrong way. And I…" She hesitated. "Well, you know my foundation helps women start over, gives them a helping hand. He was involved with someone for a long time. We helped her get on her feet when she left him last month, set her up in an apartment in Red Deer, vouched for her for a job."

Ryan straightened. "Last month?"

"Yeah, middle of the month, maybe? Definitely after Labor Day, because Sam and I sneaked away without kids for the long weekend, and it was after that. She basically left with her suitcase and that was it."

He thought back to the conversation with Andi and how she'd said she was sure Jim had been living with someone. Turned out she was right, and this woman had walked out on Jim just before the anniversary of Chelsea's death. "How did he take it?" Ryan asked. "I'm sure we didn't get a call about a domestic or anything."

"He told her to take her stuff and leave, then. Said some pretty awful stuff, but she said he never put hands on her. She said it was all psychological." Angela looked at Ryan meaningfully. "We both know there are many kinds of abuse. Either way, I got the feeling it was an unhealthy situation. I set her up with an initial counseling session in the city."

Angela was a social worker and still ran the shelter in town, along with Clara, who had once been a resident. They both knew exactly how devastating mental abuse could be.

"Anyway," Angela went on, "I know Andi's had a rough time of it, but she's probably better off without him in her life. I just hope she didn't suffer a lot of that manipulation when they were married. It was bad enough he was carrying on with their babysitter."

It was like the ground went out from beneath him. He stared at Angela for a long moment, that one last sentence echoing in his head.

"You didn't know?"

"No. Was it common knowledge?" Jim. Involved with Leslie. The threads were starting to tangle now, and where there was a tangle, there was sure to be a knot of truth.

"I don't think so."

There was too much he didn't know, but it was a starting point for further investigation. "So Jim was cheating on her with a twenty-year-old girl. He's a real piece of work."

"It looks that way. I'm glad to see her happy with you, though."

He ignored that last bit; his mind was too full of implications and possibilities. From what Andi said, Jim's put-downs had been insidious and couched in praise, just enough to keep her trying harder and feeling worse. And all the while he'd been… Ryan tamped down his anger and tried to be objective. "Do you think this woman would be open to talking to me in an official capacity?"

Angela's eyes widened in alarm. "What for? Is he in trouble? Is Andi okay?"

Ryan took a drink of his cider and held her gaze over the rim. When he lowered his cup, he said, "Just like you didn't tell me her name or any identifying details, I can't tell you that, either. But I would like to talk to her."

"I understand. I'll see what I can do."

"I appreciate it, Angela."

One of Angela's kids came around the corner, needing something, so Ryan went on his way again, his brain turning over this new information. Before long, he made his way back to Andi, who looked to be even more relaxed. "Having a good time?" he asked.

"Very. I haven't been out at all this fall. I'm glad Shelby made me come."

"Me, too. I was going to sit at home feeling sorry for myself."

"You were?"

"I've been trying to give you space."

She sighed, her smile fading. "I'm sorry about that. I really didn't mean to take my frustration out on you the other night." She hesitated, then met his gaze. "Ryan, as much as it scares me, I think you might be right about Jim. I don't understand how or why, but…"

He straightened. "What's changed your mind?"

"The daisies. No one else would know about that. The door, the tires…even running me off the road. That could have been anyone. But the photo? He would have known where to go look for that album. And he's the only one I can think of who knew about Chelsea bringing me daisies all that summer. He knew it would be a knife in my heart."

"There is one other person," he said quietly. When she merely looked at him with questions in her eyes, he added, "Leslie."

She stepped back. "Well, yes, but you can't seriously think…" She shook her head and laughed. "Les was the sweetest. She was so good to Chelsea and to all of us. She'd have no reason to hurt any of us! Least of all Chelsea. I know she loved her. Besides, losing Chelsea meant losing her job. She had nothing to gain, Ryan. It's a ridiculous idea."

"I'm sorry. I'm just trying to look at every possibility. Even the ones that seem a little out there." Ryan sighed and then remembered his mission to protect her.

"I don't want to think about it being Jim, either," she murmured. "But he always has a way of getting out of everything. Or talking you around it so you end up blaming yourself."

Ryan looked around. There were so many people nearby. "Come with me for a minute. Let's walk."

They strolled out past the barn to a small pasture where half a dozen horses grazed peacefully. Ryan rested his arms on the top railing, and Andi put her hands there, too, letting out a sigh. "This place is so gorgeous. I'm not a rancher by any means, but I can appreciate the wide-open space."

"Me, too," he answered. "Listen, I wanted to talk to you where no one else could hear us. I heard something that matches up with what you told me the other night. Jim was living with someone. She left him early in September."

Andi looked over at him, her pretty eyes widening with surprise. "Oh. Well, I didn't know for sure. I'd only heard rumors. Jim would have hated that—if she'd left him, that is. When we split, we'd been arguing a lot, and I remember thinking out loud that maybe we should call it quits." She bit down on her lip. "He said that he'd decide when it was time for it to be over. Turned out that time was only a few weeks later." She frowned. "Looking back, it was on his terms."

She swallowed and turned back toward the pasture. The light was waning now, and the moon was starting to rise. She shivered and he resisted the urge to wrap his arm around her to keep her warm.

"Was it bad, when he left?"

She nodded, not looking at him. "We'd had a huge fight. He was never physical with me, you know? But he was so—" She broke off, swallowing again, and he wondered if she was close to tears. "He was so mean. He said I was worthless. That I was a horrible wife and he deserved better. I…I believed him."

"Andi," he whispered, sympathy crowding his heart. If Jim's leaving hurt her this much, what would she do if she knew about Leslie? He couldn't bring it up. Not just because he didn't want to hurt her, but because it was now part of the investigation.

"I know he was wrong, now. But I didn't then. I was about as low as a person could get. I had lost my daughter only a year before. Then I was losing my husband. I thought I must have done something horrible to deserve what was happening. I thought it was punishment for not being a good mother or wife."

Ryan was gutted, hearing those words. Not Andi. "You were the most loving mother I've ever seen," he said softly, putting his hand over hers on the railing of the fence. "I can't speak to your marriage, but I can only imagine you tried as hard as you could."

"I did." She sniffled a little. "It took a long time for me to get over feeling like a failure. Looking back, though, I realize Jim was simply impossible to please. I'm allowed to be human. I make mistakes. But I'm not useless or uncaring."

"No, you're not," he confirmed, squeezing her fingers.

She squeezed back and something changed. Something in his heart, in his soul. He needed to take himself off this case. There was no way he could be objective now. He'd gone and fallen for her. And yet how could he back off when he knew he needed to protect her? He slid his fingers away. This—whatever was happening between them—had to wait.

"There's proof out there somewhere. I just know it. Please don't lose faith. We're going to figure this out."

"I trust you," she replied, then turned her head to look at him. "I know I said some things the other night that were harsh. I didn't want to believe it about him. I still don't, not deep down. It's so hard to wrap my head and my heart around the idea and what it really means. But I can't ignore the daisies. And yet every time I think of the possibility, my blood runs cold. I just…" She stopped.

"It might not be him," Ryan said quietly. "Give us a little more time to follow the evidence."

Silence spun out, one filled with confusion and grief. "How has this become my life?"

"When we get overwhelmed, I think that's the time we need to take it to Him," he said, pointing to the sky. "And lay our worries there."

"I know you're right." She looked over at him and smiled. "Faith means not always needing to understand. Maybe I just need a bit more of that to get me through. It's been in short supply lately. I've been so angry. But what if… I mean, I've been angry to be going through this again. But what if the purpose of all of this is to finally solve the case? What if God is really on my side?"

"God is always on our side," he replied, and smiled back.

The moon was up now, peeking through the clouds, and Ryan could see their breath in the air. "Are you cold? We could head back to the barn. Things will be going on for another hour or two."

She shrugged. "I'm chilly. But honestly, I'm ready to go home. I mean, to Shelby's. I slept great last night, but I've been sleeping so poorly lately that the thought of curling up in bed sounds so good."

"I can drive you if Shelby and Ian aren't ready to go yet."

"Are you sure?"

"Very sure," he answered, and before he could help himself, he reached out and tucked a piece of hair behind her ear.

"Ryan…"

"Shhh." He stepped back. "It's all right. I'll be the perfect gentleman."

"I never doubted it. Not once."

His heart beat double time as they made their way back to the barn. He'd see her safely home. And he was going to crack this case if it killed him.

Something had changed between them tonight, Andi realized as she followed Ryan back to the barn and the crowd that was still enjoying the music and food and wonderful company. On one hand, she was scared. Each day she wondered if the stalking was going to escalate into physical harm. And yet Ryan's words tonight had given her peace. Especially the part about having faith. She needed to remember that instead of looking inward so much.

They found Shelby and Ian. The kids wanted to stay for the fireworks that Sam and Tyson were going to set off, so she agreed to let Ryan take her home. They walked back to his truck in the dark, the chill needling her through her sweater. Once they were in the cab, he turned on the heater. "It'll warm up in a minute," he said.

"Thanks. Clear nights are cold ones. But it was worth it, for the moon and the stars." She leaned back against the seat. "I needed tonight. To get out and forget for a little while."

"I'm glad."

He turned the truck around and they started the drive to Shelby's. Instead of talking, Ryan turned the radio up just a little so music filled the cab, and he tapped his fingers on the steering wheel to the beat of the music. Andi didn't feel the need to fill up the space with chatter. Instead, she was perfectly comfortable.

The cab of the truck seemed even more intimate as they pulled into Shelby's yard. No one was home, though Andi knew that as soon as she entered the combination to the door lock, the dog would bark his head off. She liked that, actually, because it was like having an early alert system and made her feel safer. Maybe when all this was over, she'd look into getting a dog. It would be good company for her, too.

"I'll walk you to the door."

"You don't have to. I'm sure it's fine."

His gaze held hers, with only the lights from the dash illuminating the dark depths of his eyes. "Indulge me. It'll make me feel better."

"All right."

He shut off the engine and they got out. Their feet crunched over the gravel as they walked to Shelby's back door, then made hollow sounds as they climbed the wood steps to the small porch. The outside light was on, casting them in a circle of brightness. "Thank you for the drive," she said, trying to make her voice bright. Suddenly she didn't want to go in there alone. She thought about asking him to come in, making him some cocoa or…something.

"Anytime," he answered. "I'm glad we made up. I didn't like us being… I don't know. Not angry with each other, but not…" He frowned. "On the same page, I guess."

"Me, either. It's been stressful for both of us, so maybe we can cut each other a little slack."

He nodded. "I could never stay mad at you."

"Ryan…"

"I know. Everything is messy and uncertain, and my timing is all wrong. I know that. But I care about you, Andi. You must know that by now."

Oh, good heavens. Hearing him give voice to what was already in her heart made it even more difficult to reconcile. "I do," she whispered, her cheeks heating despite the cold.

And then he did something she didn't expect. He leaned forward and touched his lips to hers, lightly, but lingering enough that it was certainly no platonic peck. His lips were soft and gentle and reached into all the parts of her that needed care and patience. How did he always seem to know just what she needed?

He stepped back, his gaze stormy, and nodded at the door. "Go inside and make sure to lock the door. It's getting late, so Shelby and the kids will be home soon. And if you need anything at all, call my cell. I can be here in under five minutes."

She nodded dumbly.

"Good night, Andi."

"Night."

She fumbled her way through the combination to the keypad to the door, needing a second try to make it work. She went inside and shut the door behind her, then pushed the button to lock it again. Only after the whir of the lock did Ryan step off the porch and go back to his truck.

She pressed her fingers to her lips. He'd kissed her. He'd taken care of her tonight, not just by doing favors like before, not by being a cop, but like someone who cared about her. Who might...

No. She wasn't going to even think the word *love*.

Besides, she thought, as the dog rubbed up against her legs, welcoming her home, as nice a distraction as the evening had been, there was still someone out there who wanted to do her harm. She'd put herself first the morning that Chelsea had disappeared, and the worst had happened. Everything else could wait. Now she would put justice for her daughter first.

Chapter Thirteen

Ryan lay awake far too long into the night, thinking about that kiss, and when he woke up it was the first thing on his mind.

Only a half hour before taking her home, he'd been standing at that fence, telling himself he had to back away and do the right thing. Next thing he knew, she was looking up at him and he was moving forward and their lips were touching and he was a goner.

He'd kept it brief, simple… And yet there was nothing simple about it. From the first moment she'd called him for help, this had been building. Now the thought of anything happening to her made his heart freeze. He couldn't let that happen.

He was off shift today, then working the long Thanksgiving weekend. At least he was on the day shift. He'd be done midafternoon on Sunday, in lots of time to pick up Andi and head to his folks' place for the big turkey dinner his mom always prepared. Today his time was his own, and he was determined to spend it going through every last detail of the case. He wanted to follow up with Jim's ex, too, and hoped she'd agree to speak to them.

He got up, showered, made a massive coffee and put it in his travel mug. The best place to go over everything was at work, where reports and resources would be at his fingertips. The October day was cool and clouds had rolled in, promising a fall rain later. Ryan shivered and wondered if the rain would turn into flurries as the system came over the Rockies.

He'd unlocked his truck and was just opening the door when something crashed into his head, sending a sharp pain echoing through his skull. Then everything went dark. He thought he heard footsteps running away, crunching on the gravel of his driveway, but before he could try to turn his head, the darkness took over and he crumpled to the ground.

A dull ache centered in the back of his head, radiating toward the front. Ryan groaned and tried blinking as he came to. He lifted his head a little and realized there was gravel stuck to his cheek. He struggled to sit up and brushed at his face, the pebbles dropping to the ground. The door of his truck was still open, the dome light on. How long had he been out?

A quick check of his watch showed he'd been on the ground for twenty minutes. *Ugh.* There was a good chance he'd sustained a concussion, but whoever had been here was long gone. Once he was in a seated position, he grabbed on to the truck door handle and pulled himself to standing. Not too unsteady.

He should probably go to the clinic. His fingers probed

the lump on the back of his head, and he winced. It was a big bump but not cut. He wouldn't need stitches. All they would tell him at the clinic was that he had a concussion, tell him to take it easy, blah blah, when he knew what he really should be doing was solving this case. He'd pop a few painkillers and get to it. He had no double vision, and his feet felt pretty solid beneath him. Maybe it wasn't a concussion after all. His sister always said he had a hard head.

The big question was why he'd been attacked. As a cop, he made his fair share of enemies, it was true. But this attack? Now? It was hard to believe it would be for any reason other than this case. What had changed? Were they getting close? Hard to imagine, considering nothing seemed to be adding up.

He frowned and reached for the phone in his back pocket. He didn't want to go to the clinic to see the doctor, but he did want to make sure Andi was okay. If he'd been attacked, she might not be safe, either. As he dialed the number, he wondered if this could possibly have anything to do with last night. The only thing that had changed —the only thing—was that he'd kissed Andi last night. He'd held her hand briefly at the party. But why would that set someone off? The only way that theory worked was if Andi were being watched.

Which, considering the events of the past two weeks, was a possibility.

The clinic receptionist answered, and he asked to speak to Andi.

"She's with a patient right now. Can she call you back?"

She was at work and she was safe. She already knew to be vigilant. He didn't want to alarm her, and she was staying at Shelby's anyway, which meant after work today she'd be safe with his sister's family.

"No, that's fine. I'll catch up with her later."

After taking two pills and a glass of water, he got back in his truck and headed into town, stopping at the bakery for a dozen muffins on the way. If he was going to be at work on his day off, he might as well make the staff happy.

He put the muffins down in the lunchroom, grabbed one for himself and got to work as the pain in his head subsided a bit. To his surprise, no one seemed the least bit curious as to why he was there. Maybe his attention to the case was obvious. He was too focused to care much. Instead, he worked through the details he had, starting with the day Andi had called him to the woods where she'd found the stuffed bunny. They'd processed the scene but hadn't found much of anything, and the late-afternoon showers had made it even more difficult. He looked again at the photos of the rabbit nailed to the tree, the tests on it, the DNA results. If Jim was behind all of this, it made sense that his prints would be on it along with Chelsea's, and another set wasn't found. They'd discovered a rusty nail on the ground and half of a napkin that someone had dropped, or it had blown in, but there were no prints or anything on it. The footprints were another dead end. No one had noticed a vehicle along that road.

He pulled out a map of the area and followed the line of the trail with his finger. There was the road where they'd parked for access to the trail. He moved his finger until he got to the site where they'd found the bunny, where they'd found Chelsea. Then he moved his finger farther along the trail, headed west. It went on another four kilometers before exiting on an old logging road that had been closed for some time.

To vehicles, maybe. But not to foot traffic. And from there to the end of the logging road and the nearest road was maybe a kilometer and a half. There were no houses there, either. The odds of being seen were minuscule.

So whoever it was could have entered the trail from either end, and the chances of discovery were tiny.

What he was missing was anything actually tying Jim to the place. He was still certain Jim was the key to everything, but forced himself to look at the evidence with a critical eye and not one that necessarily supported his theory. It had to stand up.

He finished his coffee and poured another from the machine, grimacing at the slightly burned flavor.

They hadn't brought Jim in for questioning; they'd had no concrete reason to. Did he have an alibi for the day they'd discovered the rabbit? It had been warm and dry for several days before the discovery; could they even be sure when it had been left there? There were far more questions than answers.

He moved on to the Sunday night at Shelby's when Andi had been nearly run off the road. Jim's car hadn't shown any damage. They'd followed up locally, and there was no report from any of the body shops nearby about having repaired a black sedan of his make and model, but what if he'd gone farther afield? He quickly googled auto body repair for Red Deer and found twenty-seven listings. Time to do some grunt work and make some calls.

He came up blank with about fourteen, and a few were duplicate listings or dealers for a specific make. Seven said they'd get back to him. While he was waiting, he scanned the short report about the tagging of her garage door. Nothing there, either. Spray paint that could be bought at any hardware-type store. But if Jim had used the path to access her backyard, he would have been able to come and go without being seen.

The photo of Chelsea had revealed no evidence whatsoever. No fingerprints inside the house, no shoe treads, nothing. The more Ryan read through, the more frustrated he became. It seemed to him that everything was so very deliberate. Like the person—and right now, Ryan was using the name *Jim* in his head—had been wearing gloves and those silly bootees that furniture delivery people wore so they didn't track into the house.

Almost as if he'd been wearing PPE.

And with recent world events, it was no longer strange for people to have their own personal protective equipment.

A hunch was not enough to go on.

He'd been through the video footage from the strip mall, and where Andi had parked was too far away to be on camera. The most he could get was tying Jim to the area, as he was shown going in and out of the dollar store at the times the clerk had told him. Jim's car had also been parked far enough away to not be on camera. Ryan sat back in his chair. Why would someone park so far away from the one store they went into? Once again, more questions than answers.

But one final bit of footage had come in since he was last in the office, that from the bank machine. Ryan cued it up and prepared to watch.

The traffic in the vestibule was steady, but no Jim. Ryan was nearly to the end when he sat up straighter. Not Jim, but a familiar face. He paused it, zoomed in and stared.

Leslie. Leslie had also been at the strip mall that morning. He did a search and found that the car registered to her name was a red compact, but on a hunch, he dug further and discovered that her mother's car was a late-model black four-door.

Bingo.

His head started to throb again, and he went to refill his coffee as he mentally planned his next steps. He also stopped at the fridge and took out a small ice pack to put on the bump. Back in the office, he pressed it against the bump on his head and sighed. It felt good against the swelling and he closed his eyes, leaving it there for a few minutes. He popped another pill, though he was starting to feel pretty miserable. Oh, well, he could push through. He had to. Andi's safety depended on it.

His phone rang twice, with two body shops confirming they had not worked on a car of his description during the time frame he'd given them. More dead ends.

There was a knock on the door frame, and he looked up. Ben stood there, a concerned frown marring his face. "It's your day off, Ryan."

"I know," he answered, pushing back his chair and

huffing out a breath. "I came in to go over everything again, but on my own time. No overtime."

"Heck, I'm not worried about that. I'm worried about you."

"I don't need your concern. My concern is for Andi. We should have had this closed by now. Someone was in her house again, even after she changed the locks. And this morning…"

Ben's gaze sharpened. "What about this morning?"

There was no sense hiding it. He needed Ben's help, or at least his support. "Someone hit me from behind when I was getting in my truck. Knocked me out cold."

"What? And you didn't call it in?"

Ryan shook his head, but not too much because it hurt. "This is all tied together. I figure this out—" he gestured toward the desk "—and I figure out who hit me."

"But why you?"

"I can't help but think we're either getting too close in some way, or they're angry. Did you know Roxanne Fletcher went to see Andi the other day? She apologized for what happened, and Andi's sure it's not her."

"I don't think it is, either. Besides, her alibi for Chelsea's disappearance is solid. And the two cases are tied, so…"

"I'm down to two possibilities—either her ex or the babysitter. Yesterday I found out that Jim had been living with someone and she left him last month. I can't see him being happy about it. He doesn't seem the type to take rejection well."

"That's not a motive."

"Maybe not. But Andi told me he accused her of loving Chelsea more than him. He always seemed charming and perfectly fine when I saw him, but we both know it's no indication of what's going on in a marriage. What kind of man is jealous of his own kid?"

Ben came farther into the room. "What about the babysitter?"

"Rumor has it she and Jim had an affair. Also, her mother drives a black sedan. She had the opportunity. I just can't sort out a motive."

"Do you have anything concrete?"

"I've come up with some different theories, but not a single thing that ties Jim or Leslie to any of the scenes. I wish I did because then maybe we could get a warrant. The two closest things I have are that they were both present at the strip mall at the time when Andi's tires were slashed and the daisies left on her bed. That specific flower is symbolic." He rubbed his hand over his forehead. "Daisies are even engraved on Chelsea's grave marker."

Ben came closer and frowned at Ryan. "You all right?"

"Just the headache from this morning. I'll be fine. It's only been a few hours."

Ben leaned over and looked Ryan in the face. "It's six o'clock, Ryan. More than a few hours."

Ryan tried not to show his surprise. Six? He'd been here for eight hours already. How had he lost track of time? He blinked and saw gray spots before his eyes cleared again. Ben was beside him. "Let me see that bump," Ben said firmly, and Ryan knew better than to ignore that tone in his boss's voice. He dipped his head so Ben could see the back of his head.

"Ryan, how long were you out?" Ben probed the area gently. "This is big. Did you at least see the doctor?"

Ryan moved away from Ben's fingers and assessing gaze. "A few minutes. Maybe fifteen," he lied.

"Fifteen? You're probably concussed. You shouldn't even be here."

"I'm fine. The answers are here," he said, pointing at the desk. "Not here." He pointed to his head.

Ben sighed. "Okay. Let's at least get something to eat. I'll order a pizza and maybe we can work through some stuff together. I'm as frustrated with this as you are. This whole case makes me doubt my investigative abilities." He offered Ryan a sideways smile. "I don't like when a criminal makes me feel stupid."

Ryan chuckled. "No lectures?" He wasn't sure he could handle it right now. He just wanted to focus.

"No lectures. Let's sift through it all."

Ryan nodded. "I've gone through everything from the past few weeks. I'll show you what I've learned, and then maybe you can go over it again with fresh eyes while I look at the original case?"

It felt weird, making the suggestion. After all, Ben was the lead investigator. But Ben merely nodded. "You got it. I'll be back in five and we can go over what you've got."

There had to be something. It was here, in all the evidence. He knew it in his gut.

The pizza was delivered, and Ryan felt a bit better after eating. The muffin he'd had earlier hadn't been enough to sustain him, especially after losing track of time. He took a bathroom break and then sent Andi a text, checking in to make sure she was okay and safe and secure at Shelby's. She answered that she was fine and they were watching a movie with the kids and eating popcorn. Then she sent him a selfie with Macy on her lap, curled up in pajamas with a bowl of popcorn between them. It made him smile, and he wondered if she ever thought about having kids again. She had been such a good mother and could be again if she wasn't too scared. He totally understood she might be, but seeing her holding Macy did something to him. They'd only shared one kiss. How could he be thinking about a future after one single kiss?

Ben had brought in an extra chair, and Ryan quickly brought him up to speed on his ideas about access to the crime scene as well as to Andi's property. As Ben prepared to work through the details, Ryan pulled up the case from seven years ago.

He went through each piece of evidence, examined every alibi. Every witness, which wasn't many. He frowned and looked up at Ben. "Hey, Ben, that walking trail that is behind Andi's. How long has that been there?"

Ben looked up over his reading glasses and frowned as he considered. "Four, five years, maybe?"

"That's what I thought. It wasn't there when Chelsea was taken."

"Nope. It was train tracks before then. But when the trains stopped coming through town, it was converted to a walking trail."

Ryan went to work looking for a map that showed the train tracks and the area before the trail and the subsequent development that had happened in the past several years. "What if Chelsea was taken from the backyard and not the front? No one saw anything because there was nothing to see on the street side."

"We considered that she might have wandered along the tracks."

"But what if someone came to her, instead of her wandering away?"

Ben's gaze held his. "You mean someone came specifically to get her. But what are the chances that Andi would be sleeping and Chelsea was unattended at the exact right time?"

Ryan's stomach started to turn, and the gray spots appeared in front of his eyes again. He gulped in some air and tried to steady himself. "Unless the person knew. Look at Andi's statement. She said Jim left her the cold medicine on the counter that morning."

"You think he drugged her?"

"He provided the pill, and she took it. What's not in here is if it was still in the packaging or if he left it out. If he knew she was going to be passed out, he could come back and grab Chelsea while she was sleeping."

"That's a heck of a big if," Ben mused. "Most cold meds don't actually knock a person out flat."

Still, Ryan felt he was on to something. He just wished the pain in his head would go away. The sharpness was gone, but it had devolved into a kind of sick headache that made him nauseated.

He dug deeper into the original files until the type

blurred in front of his eyes from the strain. His stomach lurched and he reached for the metal garbage can beside the desk just in time.

"You've had enough for today, pal," Ben said a few moments later, pressing a cold cloth to the back of Ryan's neck. "You should get checked out."

But now that he'd thrown up, he felt a bit better. "Sorry," he mumbled, then pushed away the revolting sight of the contents of the can. He'd change the bag in a minute.

Except it made him pause. He straightened, took a swig of water from the bottle he had sitting on the desk and scrolled through the reports until he got to the autopsy report.

Chelsea's stomach contents. Orange juice. Vodka. And doughnuts, specifically a plain yeast doughnut.

He flipped through again and looked at Jim's statement. Chelsea had disappeared sometime in a ninety-minute window that morning. A supplier of Jim's had confirmed that they'd been on a sales call that morning. Then Jim had headed back to Cadence Creek, stopping at a gas station to fill up along the way. The gas receipt was stamped at 9:22 a.m., and Jim had reported Chelsea missing at seven after ten. Forty-five minutes later.

In the report, Jim had said it took him twenty minutes to get home, which would have put his arrival at the house at nine forty-two, give or take a minute or so. That left twenty-five minutes unaccounted for.

Twenty-five minutes was not enough to arrive, take Chelsea, go to the woods and return home. Ryan slumped over the desk, but only for a moment. He quickly googled the gas station and frowned. "Hey, Ben, didn't there use to be a coffee shop at the gas station off Highway 22?"

"Yeah, there was. When it changed hands, they closed it. I used to get breakfast sandwiches there all the time."

Breakfast sandwiches, sure. But also doughnuts. And orange juice. What if, instead of going home first, Chelsea had already been in the car?

Suddenly inspired, Ryan flipped through to the forensics report on the crime scene. There'd been vomit found close to the body. "Ben," he said, his voice tight with anticipation. "Ben."

"You find something?"

"Yeah. I think I did." When Ben came around the corner of the desk, Ryan pointed, trying to stay calm and not get ahead of himself. "Chelsea's stomach contents. It showed she'd recently eaten doughnuts and orange juice. And vodka." They'd had the working theory all along that her killer had given her alcohol to sedate her. It wouldn't take much for a three-year-old. "But the vomit they found at the scene… It's slightly different. We missed it, Ben. It was right there, and we missed it. Orange juice and doughnut and—" he tapped the monitor "—egg and English muffin. The killer had her in the car when they stopped for doughnuts. When he dosed her with vodka. When he ate his own sandwich." He turned his gaze to Ben's face. "When he stopped for gas at nine twenty-two."

Just then, Ryan's phone rang, and he reached for it, answering blindly. "Ryan Davenport."

He reached for a pen and scribbled down the information, then clicked off the phone. "On September

twentieth, a body shop in Red Deer did some small repair work on a black sedan with the license plate match-
ing Jim Wallace's."

Ben's mouth broke into a grin. "Finally, a break. It's
not enough—"

"But it's a break," Ryan said. "It's enough to bring
him in for questioning."

"It is," Ben replied, putting a hand on Ryan's shoulder. "I'll get on it. You need to go home. You've been
working for hours. We'll pay him a visit in the morning."

Ryan didn't really want to wait, but he knew Ben
was right. He needed some downtime. Still, for the first
time, Ryan felt hopeful. For justice for Chelsea, and for
Andi's safety.

Chapter Fourteen

After a massive breakfast of chocolate chip pancakes and bacon, Andi said goodbye to the kids, promising to return that afternoon with all the fixings to make homemade pizzas for dinner. It was her treat, since Shelby had made dinner for the past few nights and had made Andi feel so welcome even though she had her own household to run. Her best friend said it was no bother, but Andi couldn't take advantage forever. Thanksgiving dinner was Sunday at the Davenport family home, with Shelby and Ryan's folks. After that, she was going back to her own place.

But she hadn't packed enough clothes, and last night Gillian had spilled juice on Andi's pj's, so this morning she was going home to get some fresh clothes and do a load of laundry. But first, she'd head to the grocery store to pick up what she needed to make pizzas with the kids for dinner. She'd even got Carson and Macy to agree to help clean up the mess so Shelby could have a real break.

The weather was gorgeous, and she tapped her fingers on the steering wheel with the music on the radio as she drove home. She hadn't heard anything from Ryan until last night, when he'd texted and she'd sent the selfie. He'd messaged back Wish I was there and she had, too. They hadn't spoken since the kiss on the doorstep on Thursday, but the memory of it was like a sweet little morsel, tucked in the back of her mind, there to retrieve whenever she got overwhelmed with the events of the past few weeks.

The grocery store was busy for a Saturday morning, and Andi grabbed a shopping cart and started making her way down the aisles. She was waiting in line to check out when she heard her name and turned to find Leslie headed her way.

"Hey, sweetie," she said, offering a smile.

"Hi. I'm glad I found you. Do you have time to talk?"

An uneasy feeling spread through Andi's stomach, though she couldn't explain why. "Maybe? I have a busy day, though."

"It won't take long." Leslie's voice was low, and her bubbly personality was absent. "I just… There are things I need to say to you, and I can't wait any longer. Please?"

That slow, sickening dread settled in her gut once more. "Um…okay. Want to go back to my place?"

Leslie shook her head quickly. "No. I mean…" She hesitated and fidgeted with her hands. "There's a picnic table outside where the staff sometimes sits for their smoke breaks. Is that okay?"

Outside in public. Andi wasn't sure what she was

so nervous about. "Okay. Let me pay for these and put them in my car first."

The four minutes it took to check out and put the bags in her car seemed to take forever, but she went to the side of the store and found Leslie sitting at the picnic table, one knee bouncing up and down. The girl was nervous, but why?

Andi slid onto the seat across from Leslie. "Okay, hon, you'd better tell me what's going on. You're scaring me a little. Are you in some kind of trouble?"

Leslie shook her head, and when she looked up at Andi, there were tears in her eyes. "No. At least, I'm not now. But I was. I should have told you this long ago."

"Told me what?" Andi asked, her voice cautious.

"When I worked for you…that summer before Chelsea…" She stopped, bit on her lip. "I'm so ashamed, Andi. So scared to say it."

Andi reached over and took her hand. "It's okay. Whatever it is, it's okay." Andi struggled to keep the tremor out of her voice. Whatever Leslie needed to share wasn't going to be pleasant.

"I had an… What I mean to say is…" She took a big breath and let it out. "Okay. Andi, Jim and I had an affair."

Andi sat back as if slapped. "You what?"

"I know. It's so awful. I was young and stupid and he was older and I was flattered and he told me things that…that made me feel sorry for him. I'm so, so sorry, Andi."

Andi tried to remain steady. In a way, this changed nothing. "Jim and I divorced anyway. I guess I shouldn't be surprised…at him, not you, Leslie. He was older and your boss. You were young and naive. He took advantage."

Leslie sniffled and looked at Andi with tortured eyes. "That's not all of it," she whispered.

There was more? Andi swallowed tightly, understanding the girl needed to get this off her chest, but Andi wasn't sure how much more she could take.

"That July I found out I was pregnant," she said, and then slid her gaze away. "When I told Jim, he told me to get rid of it. But I couldn't, you know? And then… I lost the baby. The doctor said it happens a lot, more than people realize. But it was still rough."

"Of course it was." She looked at Leslie with new sympathy. "I had two miscarriages of my own. It's awful. Who knew besides Jim?"

"No one." Leslie had her hands together now and was fiddling with her thumbs. "I went to work and cared for Chelsea and just tried to hide how mixed-up and sad I was."

Guilt slid through Andi. "I never noticed. How could I have missed it? I'm sorry, Leslie."

"Why would you be sorry? I slept with your husband!" She lowered her voice again. "I told myself it was no less than I deserved. But when Chelsea died…" She shuddered and sniffed again. "I'd been trying to work up the courage to put in my notice. It was so hard. Jim broke things off in August when I told him I wouldn't have an abortion. It was awful, being in your house. The bright spot was Chelsea. She was something." A smile flirted with her lips for a moment and then was gone again. "After she died, Jim came to me and accused me of taking her. Said that it was revenge on him for breaking things off and for losing the baby."

"And did you?" Andi asked, her heart in her throat. "Did you take her?"

"No! Oh, Andi, no. She was the one bright thing in my life. I was heartbroken when she disappeared. I spent most of the fall in my room and then went to Calgary to school for the winter term. I couldn't be here anymore. Not after everything I'd done."

With the confession over, they sat in silence for several moments, absorbing, coming to terms with all that had been revealed. Andi had already come to grips with the fact that Jim had not been a good husband. That he'd been overly critical and verbally abusive. But this…this was something else entirely. He'd been unfaithful. He'd targeted a young girl and exploited her. And then, in typical Jim fashion, he found a way to turn it around and make it into her fault.

"Leslie, can I offer you some advice?" she finally said.

"I don't deserve it. You should hate me right now."

Andi thought about that and then looked at Leslie. "I don't hate you. I forgive you." It was true, she realized. The sense of betrayal she had expected didn't exist. Perhaps because they'd both been victims of the same man.

Leslie started crying again, wiping her eyes with her fingers.

"Les, someone has been following me, trying to scare me. I don't want the same to happen to you, so be careful, okay? Be aware of your surroundings until the police can figure out who is behind it."

She nodded quickly.

"I don't want to scare you. I just want you to be safe."

"I'm spending the weekend at home anyway," she said. "But thank you. It's so much more than I deserve."

Andi smiled and touched Leslie's hand again. "Listen, let me give you one more bit of advice, from the voice of experience. It gets better when you can learn to forgive yourself. Ask God for forgiveness and it'll be granted. Forgiving yourself is the hardest part."

"Thank you, Andi. I feel…lighter. Awful, but lighter."

"Don't let him take anything more away from you," Andi said, getting up from the table. "Now, I've got ice cream in the car that's going to need putting in the freezer right away. You're okay now?"

Leslie nodded. "I'm okay."

With one last pat on her hand, Andi started walking to her car. She hoped no one could tell how her legs were shaking or that she was on the verge of crying.

He'd called her a failure, but he'd broken their vows.

She no longer thought he was incapable of anything, because with Leslie's confession came one very large truth: she'd never really known Jim at all.

Twenty minutes later, Andi pulled into her driveway, turning down the radio as she slowed and scanned the area for anything out of place. Nothing that she could see. Anxiety balled in the pit of her stomach; returning to her house, the place that was supposed to be her safe space and refuge, now filled her with fear and uncertainty. For the first time, she looked at it and horrible visions of what had happened under her roof raced through her brain. Jim and Leslie, together. In her house. In her bed.

Before she got out of the car, she grabbed her phone and sent Ryan a quick message, asking him to meet her as soon as he could, and then slid the phone into her jacket pocket. Then she grabbed her overnight bag and purse and headed toward the door. She had family and friends to stay with, a good job, food on the table. She could support herself now, and for that she was grateful. She put the key in the lock while still counting her blessings.

The house was quiet, and she dropped her bag and purse as she toed off her shoes in the entry. Humming softly, she hung up her car keys and then reached for her bag. A hot shower was going to feel wonderful.

She'd taken all of six steps when she caught movement out of the corner of her eye. Her heart froze as she turned her head and saw Jim sitting in her living room, facing the hallway, his eyes on her and his lips curved in a smile that made her blood run cold.

"Jim. My goodness, you scared me." She would try as hard as she could to keep things level and not panic. "What are you doing here?"

He got up and everything in her told her to run, but she knew she wouldn't get far. Jim was taller, and he'd catch her before she ever got out the door. Better to placate him, pretend nothing was wrong.

He reached into his pocket, took out her brand-new

key and threw it on the hardwood floor. "You changed the locks."

She swallowed, then gave a small nod and lied. "I broke off a key in the lock, so I had them replaced last week."

"Really."

She nodded again. "Yes. Where did you find the key? I lost it the first night. I'm so glad to have it again." She looked into his eyes. "You just never know who might use a lost key to break in."

He smiled again, and she tried not to shudder. "Like I did?"

Breathe, Andi. Keep breathing. "Well, you're not a stranger, now, are you? We spent a lot of years together," she said, hoping that appealing to the early days of their marriage would calm him. She really just wanted him to leave. "What can I help you with? I mean, why did you come over? Did you remember something you left behind?"

Her plan failed utterly, because he took three steps and was there in front of her, reaching out to grab her arm. His grip was firm and painful, and she winced before she could stop herself. His smile grew.

"Yeah," he said. "You."

Ryan was with Sergeant Rogers when they went to Jim's just before eight o'clock. Ben knocked at the door and identified himself, but there was no answer. He knocked again, and Ryan frowned. "I'll have a peek in the garage," he suggested, and went down the steps to the detached garage. He peered in the window, and while the glare made it difficult to see, it was clear that there was no car inside.

"Car's gone," he called back to Ben.

Ben descended the steps. "We can try his workplace. A lot of dealers are open on Saturdays."

Ryan shaded his eyes and pressed his face close to the glass again. The garage was very, very neat. Across from the window was a steel shelving unit containing several jugs and cans. Ryan wondered if there happened to be a can or two of black spray paint. But without a search warrant, he couldn't go inside.

And tagging someone's garage wasn't really worthy of an indictable mischief charge. Not on its own.

Frustration mounted again, and Ryan sighed, touching the back of his head. The pain was better today, but he still wasn't feeling great. He wouldn't show that to Ben, though. As his supervisor, Ben would likely make him see a doctor and go home until cleared for work again.

"Let's head into his place of work, see if he's there," Ben suggested. "I'll give the Red Deer detachment the heads-up."

Ryan agreed because it was the place that made the most sense, but he didn't get a warm and fuzzy feeling about it. Maybe it was the head injury, maybe it was not having seen Andi for a few days and worrying about her, but his gut was saying something was wrong. "Okay," he agreed. "If he's not there, we'll make a new plan."

What he really wanted to do was call Andi to make sure she was okay, but he couldn't do that in front of

Ben. He was already skating on thin ice and could be in a lot of trouble if Ben knew how close he and Andi had become.

He got back in the passenger side of the car and prepared for the drive, but as they pulled away from the driveway, he looked back over his shoulder at the house.

Something was wrong. And not knowing what was driving him up the wall.

"What do you mean, me?" Andi asked, fear now taking hold. Ryan had been right, hadn't he? She struggled to think clearly. Had to come up with a way to escape or…something. She pulled against his grip, hoping he would ease his hold, but his fingers tightened around her bicep.

"Sit down, Andi."

It wasn't a suggestion. The threat in his voice was clear, and she swallowed against the panic fighting its way to the surface. Panic would not solve a single thing. She took one step to the side so that her calves were against a chair, and she sat. She immediately regretted it. Jim was now towering in front of her, his height demonstrating his position of power over her.

"Jim, I don't understand what's happening," she said, her voice wobbling. "Why are you doing this?" She had to keep him talking. Give Ryan a chance to get her message. She could not think about Leslie right now. Giving in to the emotion and rage wouldn't be helpful.

"Seriously?" He barked out a laugh and she cringed at the loud sound. "Oh, Andi. You always were a little stupid, weren't you? Or are you just playing dumb?"

She looked around the room, searching for any sort of an escape route. Jim was between her and the hall. He had her cornered.

"What are you looking for, your lover?"

Her gaze snapped up as her lips fell open. "What are you talking about?"

"Don't play innocent with me. You and the cop. I know you're a thing. He's always hanging around. At first I thought maybe he was just being helpful. Then he kissed you the other night. Don't worry. He paid for touching what's mine. Got a good knock on the head for it, too."

Andi tucked her hands under her legs so he couldn't see them shake. He'd hurt Ryan? She didn't have to ask. It seemed Jim was happy to give her the details.

"He didn't even see me coming. A hit to the back of the head and he dropped like a rock."

Fear rushed through her. Was he saying that he'd killed Ryan? She thought a hasty prayer. *Dear Lord, please let Ryan be alive.*

Jim chuckled. "He's going to have a headache for quite a while with the lump I gave him." He aimed his dark glare at Andi. "That'll teach him for interfering."

He was alive. Relief replaced the fear and she wondered how long she could ride this roller coaster of emotion. She had to keep herself together and use her head. That was the only chance she had to get out of this situation. "Interfering in what?" she asked. "Jim, please help me understand. What's going on?"

He pointed at her, his eyes glittering viciously. "You. And her. Treating me like I'm something to ignore and throw away." He cursed loudly and she cringed at the hateful words. "You think you're better than everyone else. Funny, because you could never get anything right. I put up with a lot from the two of you."

Was he talking about her and Chelsea? But Chelsea had been just a baby!

"Now she's gone and left me, too. Walked out like she didn't have a care in the world." He cursed again, calling "her" a nasty name. Was he talking about the woman he'd been living with?

She tried placating again. "The woman who was living with you? I'm sorry, Jim. You must have cared for her a lot. Maybe you can work things out."

He snorted. "Nice try. She's worthless, just like you. Self-centered, only thinking of herself. Remember, I'm the one who gets to say when it's over. Get up."

Andi hesitated, puzzled. She paused a little too long, because he reached out and yanked her to her feet. "I said get up!"

He was so close to her she could smell his breath. It smelled like coffee and something else, something stronger. Some sort of alcohol.

"I—I'm up," she murmured, her body shaking. "Let me go."

The only response she got was a punch to the stomach.

The air rushed out of her as she doubled over, gasping. Pain radiated from her abdomen down her legs and she tried to draw breath, but it wouldn't come. She dropped to her knees and curled up until the air came back in a rush. He'd never, ever hit her before. This wasn't the Jim she'd been married to. Except it was. It was the Jim he was capable of being, and she'd never seen it. How could she have been so blind?

He pulled her to her feet again, and she knew his fingers were going to leave bruises. Her thoughts of all he'd done threatened to overwhelm her. She would deal with that later. Right now she had to stay alive. She had to use her brain to not only get out of this situation but to make sure Jim didn't get away.

She lifted her chin, not too much, not as a challenge, but to try to make a connection, no matter how sick the thought made her. This was the man who'd been playing mind games with her. The man who... She would not cry out at the thought. The man who had murdered his own daughter. She accepted the truth now. Why? She had to know why. And how.

"Please," she entreated softly. "I just want to help."

He snorted again, and she watched with some fear as he flexed his fingers into a fist again, then relaxed. "Help?" He laughed as if it were a hilarious joke. "When have you ever considered me? Once you had Chelsea, it was like I didn't exist. You got what you wanted, and you certainly didn't need me anymore. And what did I do? Worked my fingers to the bone, keeping you in this house, keeping both of you. Moneybags. That's all I was to you."

She shook her head. "That's not true. I—"

He slammed his hand on the entertainment unit, the flat of his palm making a terrible noise on the solid wood. "It is true! You only had eyes for her. But don't worry. I got attention elsewhere."

He didn't elaborate and she kept her mouth shut so she wouldn't set him off. The truth was, after her maternity leave, they'd both worked full-time, and she'd contributed to the household just fine. She'd adored her daughter, but every day she'd tried to make time for Jim and their marriage, even when she was dog-tired. The truth was suddenly so clear. Blaming herself had been a waste of time. Nothing would have made Jim happy. He wanted—needed—to be the center of attention. As far as working himself to the bone, he was a sales rep for agricultural equipment. It was a good job and he worked hard, but it was no more tiring than any other occupation and a lot less than some.

Jim had his own reality in his head. She realized that now. And she really didn't know how to navigate that reality.

What she wouldn't give for Ryan to burst through her door. She didn't like the thought of needing to be saved, but at this moment she was willing to surrender to that thought. She was in over her head. But how in the world could she get help?

Jim pulled her out of the living room and into the kitchen. "Put on your shoes," he ordered. "And get your keys. We're going for a drive."

Everything in her told her she should not get in a car with Jim and especially not drive to another location. She turned to face him and say so, but any protest faded from her lips as she came face-to-face with a gun.

Chapter Fifteen

When Jim's place of work turned up another dead end, Ben and Ryan returned to the detachment. Meanwhile, the other officers on duty were told to keep their eyes open for Jim and his car.

A sense of unease settled low in Ryan's gut. Before heading out in his patrol car, he took a moment to check his texts. There was one from his sister, updating him on what she and Andi had planned for the day and asking him to join them for pizza.

He was going to leave it at that when his phone rang. It was Shelby. "Hey, kiddo," he said, trying to make his voice light. "Just got your message."

"Have you heard from Andi today?"

"No. Why?"

"I texted her about picking up a few extra things and haven't heard back. Normally it wouldn't bother me, but with everything that's going on…"

He sighed and flexed his neck. The dull ache still hadn't gone away.

"Ry, are you okay?"

"Not really. I took a hit to the head yesterday." He suddenly realized he'd overlooked something important. "Shel, do you guys still keep the trail cam going?"

"Sure. Especially this time of year. The kids love checking it for wildlife."

"Can you do me a favor?" He'd been hit on the head the morning after he'd kissed Andi. Certainly her movements had been followed the past few weeks. If Jim had seen him kiss her, that could have provoked him into attacking Ryan. "Can you go back to Thursday night between eight thirty and nine? And tell me if you see anything?"

"You think someone saw you drop Andi off?"

"Yeah. And saw me kiss her good-night. Please, just take a look at the camera and let me know the moment you've watched it."

"I'll do it right now." Anxiety tinged her voice. "Are you going to check on her?"

"Yeah, I am. I'll keep you updated."

They hung up and he frowned and messaged Andi again.

Can you check in with me so I know you're okay?

He didn't want to alarm her, but nothing about this was sitting right. He'd just head over to her place and check on her.

A frown permanently in place on his face, he headed out to the lot where his car waited. He was just putting on his seat belt when his phone buzzed with a new message.

"That was fast," he muttered, but when he looked at the screen, the message was from Andi, not Shelby.

I have new information. Can you meet me at my place ASAP? A.

He threw the phone on the seat and put the car in gear.

"Leave your purse. Keys only."

Andi flinched at the harsh tone and reached for the keys on the hook. Her hand shook as she clutched the ring. Being on the receiving end of a punch was horrible enough; staring at the black barrel of a handgun was infinitely worse. Jim was unhinged, and she couldn't take the chance that the gun was just for show. She left her purse on the bench and slid her feet into her shoes.

"Out the door and lock it."

She obeyed but brushed her hand over the pocket of her light fleece that she'd worn from Shelby's. She'd left her purse behind, but her phone wasn't in her purse. It was in her pocket. If she could find a way to place a call... If she could distract him even for a moment... Unlikely, since his gaze never left her. She shivered. She'd figure it out. She had to.

"Give me the keys."

She handed them over, and he used the fob to unlock her doors. He followed her down the steps and to her car, his gun poking into her side. Once at the car, he opened her door and pushed her in the driver's side. She couldn't go anywhere since he still had the keys, but in the time it took for him to shut her door and walk around the hood, she grabbed her phone, pressed the buttons on the side and swiped for an emergency call. She tucked the phone back in her pocket and hoped he didn't hear the operator pick up. It was her only hope right now.

Jim got in the car, slammed the door and handed her the keys. "Drive."

She started the engine while saying, "Where are we going? Where are you taking me?"

"You're the one doing the driving. Shut up, Andi. You're going to shut up and I'm going to talk now. And you're going to listen."

"Just don't hurt me, Jim, please. Please put away the gun."

"Shut up and drive!" he exploded. "Let's go, now!"

She put the car in Reverse and backed out of the driveway, looking both ways before turning onto the street, hands shaking on the wheel. She hoped the call had gone through. With Jim commanding her to drive, she couldn't quite make out if anyone had picked up on the other end. But she was determined to make sure she said things that would alert someone to their situation and location. As a plan it was feeble, but it was the best one she had.

"Go out here and turn left."

She obeyed, putting on her turn signal and stopping at the stop sign. Inside, her heart was quaking. She was driving but Jim was in control. Wherever they were going, she was pretty sure he didn't intend for her to come back. For a moment she pondered heaven and wondered if Chelsea would be there. Her eyes pricked with tears. Then she thought of Ryan, and Shelby, and her parents, and even Shelby's children. She didn't want to leave yet. She wanted to live. For a while she hadn't really cared if she lived or died, but she suddenly realized that she had something to live *for*. Her family. Friends. She thought of Ryan. Maybe even love again. Wasn't that something?

"You were the one who left the daisies on my bed," she said, knowing she had to keep talking in case the operator was listening. "But what I don't understand is how you got in after the locks were changed."

"You saved me a lot of time and bother," he said, clearly pleased with himself. "You dropped one of the new keys off your key ring. It was right there, in front of the bottom step. I was going to put the flowers at your door if I couldn't find a way in. But this was better. Did it freak you out, finding them there?"

Ugh, he sounded so self-satisfied. But she wanted to keep him talking, so she told the truth. "Yes. Yes, it did. And the photo?"

"I had the old keys copied when I left. That one was easy. I bet you wondered if you were going a little bit crazy." His grin was wide. "Wondered if you'd taken the picture out yourself but couldn't remember. You were always doing things and then forgetting about it after."

Her cheeks burned as she understood his words for what they were: classic gaslighting. How many times had he pulled this trick on her when they were married? She wasn't sure if it made her angry or disgusted. Everything in her wanted to contradict him, to tell him she was done with his abuse and manipulation. But one glance at the gun, still trained on her side, made her reconsider.

She would have to choose her moment.

"Turn here and go west."

Her heart dropped at the new instruction. She knew where they were going now, and if there was any chance that there was someone on the other end of her phone, she had to say it out loud. "You're taking me to the woods. To where…" Her throat tightened. "To where Chelsea was killed."

His face twisted into something ugly. "Enough talking. Keep your hands on the wheel and your eyes straight ahead."

She chanced a glance at him and then looked back at the road, at the ditch along the side. All she'd have to do was put the car off the road and his plan would be shot. But then, she wasn't sure she could outrun him, and she might get hurt. It was too risky.

"Don't even think about it," Jim said, as if he could read her thoughts. "If you want to know what really happened to our daughter, you'll do exactly as I say. Otherwise, you'll never know. Never."

He knew exactly what to say to get her to comply. Because she wanted answers after all this time. And even if it killed her, she was going to get them.

Ryan drove in the yard and saw that Andi's car was gone. It was too quiet. He knocked on the door but there was no answer. Had she gone back to Shelby's? He texted her and then walked the perimeter of the backyard and found the narrow path where Jim had been accessing the property. It looked as though the grass was freshly crushed, and Ryan followed it, through the tall, dry grass and shrubs to the walking path. The path went to the left for a good mile or more, but he knew that to the right it backed onto a cul-de-sac in a newer development. He trotted down that way, his shoes crunching on the crusher dust. He passed a couple walking their dog, offering a good morning, and kept on until he reached the end where the trail met pavement again.

Jim's car was parked at the curb.

His cell rang, and he lifted it to find Shelby's name on the display. "Did you find anything?" he asked.

"Ryan." Shelby's voice shook. "Yeah, I found something. It was Jim. I'm sure of it. Watching right at the edge of the lawn, by the trees with the bird feeders. It's dark and it's grainy, but I swear to you, Jim was watching you that night."

"Don't erase it," he ordered. "Make a copy if you can and email it to my work address."

"You got it. Have you found Andi?"

"Not yet. I thought she might be with you."

"No. Oh, dear. What can I do?"

"Pray," Ryan said, and then clicked off the phone.

He was nearly back to the path to her property when his radio crackled for all units. When he answered, he recognized Sherry, one of the dispatchers. He told her to go ahead, but he wasn't prepared for what she said.

"...the call is ongoing. Andi says they're going to where their daughter was killed."

He broke into a run. "I'm at her place now. I'll be en route in one minute. Suspect's car is located on the Spruce Creek cul-de-sac."

"Suspect is considered armed and dangerous."

"Copy that." His heart went to his throat.

Response from the other officers confirmed he was closest, and so he raced back to his car and peeled out of the driveway, using lights and sirens. He should have figured this out sooner. They should have picked Jim up last night. Recriminations bounced around inside his head, but he focused on shoving them aside. He needed to keep his head about him and keep her safe.

He just hoped she could hold on.

Andi swallowed tightly as she parked the car where Jim indicated. It seemed like a horrible joke that the October day was perfectly stunning while her life was in danger. She got out of the car, and Jim immediately came around and gripped her by the arm, tugging her toward the shallow ditch. Pain radiated to her shoulder as she stumbled along.

"Ow, you're hurting me," she said, as he pushed her toward the edge of the trail.

He let go of her arm and nudged her forward with a push to the back. "Keep moving."

She tripped and then got her footing. "I did what you asked. I came with you. Now you need to tell me everything. You said you would."

"When we get there."

She frowned. She could have an opportunity here. The trail ran for quite a way and all she would have to do was start running and she could escape. The chances of a bullet hitting her as she ran were greatly reduced, but she stayed where she was because she wanted to know. She wanted to know what had happened to Chelsea, but more than that, she wanted to know *why*.

What would be so awful that someone would kill their own daughter?

The leaves were pretty much gone from the trees now, and Andi could see the clear blue sky above. The trail was covered with the dried leaves, crunching under their feet as they moved deeper into the forest. A couple of squirrels chattered to each other but fell silent as Andi and Jim neared the spruce trees where they were playing. Andi's heart beat a fast, fearful rhythm, but she was hanging on, staying calm, trying to keep her head about her. Praying someone picked up on her car and had alerted the authorities.

The clearing was not far away now, and her steps slowed. Jim nudged her back again with the hard barrel of the gun, and she jumped forward. "We're nearly there," she said, trying to keep the wobble out of her voice. "You can tell me now what you wanted to say."

"I'll say it when I'm good and ready," he snapped.

They made it to the edge of the clearing, and Andi's heart stopped for a moment. The last time she'd been here, the stuffed rabbit had been nailed to the birch tree. She could still see it there in her mind, the soft floppy ears dangling lifelessly. Chelsea's favorite, the one thing she never left home without. Andi half turned and stared up at Jim. It was so hard to look at him now, knowing everything he'd done, trying to reconcile it with the man she'd thought she knew. The man who had fathered her child. Who had taken vows with her in the church on a sunny June Saturday.

"The stuffed rabbit. Why?" The last word came out choked, and she swallowed against her dry throat.

To her surprise, what appeared to be pain flitted across his features. "Because she was my daughter, too. And I had nothing left of her."

Andi wrenched away, anger filling the spot where fear had been living. "Nothing left of her? You took her life! Do you understand how absurd that sounds?"

"Don't talk to me about absurd!" he yelled. He shook the gun, motioning toward the tree. "Go over there. Do it now, or I'll shoot you."

She lifted her chin. "You're going to shoot me anyway, aren't you? So what if I don't do as you say?"

He reached out and grabbed her chin with his free hand, squeezing until she whimpered. "You're right. But the question is, do you want to know what happened to your daughter or not? And, Andi? You putting up a fight just means I'm going to take my time and do it slower." He tapped the gun on her thigh. "Maybe the leg first. Or the arm." He released her chin and then ran his hand down to her neck. "Maybe I'll do that to slow you down." His fingers tightened around her throat, and she felt sick to her stomach. Would he kill her the way he'd killed their child?

She had to buy more time. First of all, she wanted his confession. "Fine," she said, and he released her.

"By the tree. Hands where I can see them."

He grabbed her wrist and tugged her over to the birch tree, then pushed her shoulders so her back was flat against the trunk. As he moved away, his arm glanced against her jacket and he paused. "What's in your jacket?"

Cold fear seized her. "Nothing."

He reached in, his gaze holding hers, and took out her phone. "Your phone?" he shouted in her face.

"You told me to leave my purse. I left the house as I was."

He pulled back with his shoulder and threw the phone into the dense brush. And then he rewarded her with a slap to the face.

It felt as if her eye exploded as the impact shuddered across her jaw and cheekbone. Instinctively she raised her hand to the side of her face as her vision blurred and she struggled to stay upright.

Her phone was gone, and with it, the only link she might have had to help.

Ryan slammed his hand against the steering wheel as he sped toward the service road closest to the clearing where Chelsea had been found. The emergency call from her phone had been dropped, not that he was surprised. Service in that part of the woods was sketchy at the best of times. At least he knew where they were going and that Jim was armed. His colleagues wouldn't be far behind him. But he wasn't waiting.

He shut off his lights and pulled behind Andi's car,

then radioed in the location. "I'm approaching from the east, at the trailhead," he advised.

"Seven minutes out," came the call from another officer.

In seven minutes, he could be on scene.

In seven minutes, Andi could be dead.

Chapter Sixteen

"You are all the same," Jim growled. Andi wondered how on earth she could have ever found him handsome and gentle. His face was now contorted with anger and viciousness. "You, Caroline, even Leslie. Always causing trouble." He wiped his hand over his face while Andi stood still, using the trunk of the birch for support. Her head was still ringing from the slap.

"Caroline...the woman you were living with?"

"She turned out to be as useless as you," he snapped. "More concerned with going out with friends and buying new things, as if I couldn't provide for her. As if I wasn't enough. Like I didn't even exist."

Andi gaped at him. That was what this was all about? He wasn't enough?

"What does Leslie have to do with this?" she asked. She wanted to hear him say it. Needed to.

"Oh, sweet Leslie," he said, his voice silky smooth. "She was lovely, until she stopped doing what she was told. Remember, I get to say when it's over. I did with her, too."

Andi didn't react and was gratified when Jim's eyebrows drew together.

"What, you thought I didn't know?" she said. He didn't need to know she'd found out only an hour and a half ago. "I know all about it. About the baby."

He came forward and slapped her again. It hurt, but she wasn't sorry she'd claimed those few moments of power. It might have been foolish, but it was also buying her time.

He started to pace in front of her. "You want to know what happened? I'll tell you." He stopped pacing and stared her in the face, his cold eyes freezing her soul. "I had this whole plan. To make you see me again. It was always about her."

"Our daughter," she clarified.

"Yes, our daughter." His voice caught, surprising her.

"You cared about her, too," she suggested, hoping that if he calmed, he'd stop waving a loaded gun around.

"Of course I did!" he shouted. "She was my kid. And she was innocent, I knew that. But then she had to ruin everything. Why do women always ruin everything?" He pressed his hand to his forehead as he let out a strange sound. The ball of fear and anxiety in Andi's stomach tightened.

"I'm sure she didn't mean to," Andi said softly.

He glared at her. "You played your part perfectly, just as I planned. The cold, the medicine… You were so trusting and gullible. It was nothing to swap the cold tablet with a sleeping pill. It never takes much medication with you. I knew you'd be out within half an hour."

"You drugged me." Her mouth dropped open. She'd hated herself for falling asleep so easily that day. She was a nurse. She should have realized it wasn't right. But with Chelsea gone, everything had turned upside down.

"Of course I did. And came back to get Chelsea."

"Why? Why would you do that?"

He started pacing again. "She wasn't supposed to wake up. She wouldn't stop crying."

"What are you talking about, Jim? What happened?"

He walked to the edge of the clearing, and Andi fought the urge to run. Her brain was shouting at her to escape while she could. But her feet remained rooted to the ground. She needed to know the rest.

"I had a meeting that morning with a client—that much was true. But I did it from the car, on the way home. You were sound asleep when I got back, passed out on the couch. Chelsea was on the floor, watching the end of the movie you'd put on for her. It was no trouble for me to tell her to join me for doughnuts and let Mommy sleep."

Andi's stomach lurched. How well he'd orchestrated everything.

"I wasn't going to kill her." His voice broke and he looked away. "I wouldn't have done that! I was just gonna leave her out here. There's an old shack about ten minutes more down the trail. I was going to put her in there and then find her again. I was going to be the hero, don't you see?" He punctuated his words with colorful curses that made Andi blink. Jim had never been one to swear before, but clearly she'd never really known him.

"You were going to leave her and then find her again?" Andi tried to sort through what he'd said. To be a hero. "So you could be her rescuer?"

"So you would look at me like I was something!" he shouted at her again. "Instead of just being a paycheck at the end of the week to buy diapers and bread. I'd be the guy who saved your daughter!"

"I never thought of you that—"

"Shut up! You did!"

She quieted, needing him to settle a little. This was all because he'd been jealous of his own child. Because all of Andi's attention hadn't been on him. It was hard to wrap her head around.

"I gave her vodka in her orange juice, so she wouldn't remember anything," he continued. "And her bunny to keep her company while she was out here. She fell asleep right there in her car seat. Only she woke up when we were coming through the woods. She wouldn't stop screaming." His pacing increased and he moved his arms, clearly agitated. Andi held her breath. "I only wanted to make her be quiet, don't you see? She just needed to be quiet and sleep a little longer. I didn't mean for it to happen. She ruined the whole plan. And then she just... She stopped breathing."

Andi felt her heart break in two all over again. A howl of grief formed in her chest, but she didn't let it out. She would not give Jim the satisfaction of watching her fall apart a second time. But her body quivered with the effort of holding it in. Her precious baby, and the man who had sworn to love and protect them both. When Chelsea died, Andi had thought there couldn't be anything worse. Now she knew there was.

Jim came close again, close enough his breath was in her face and his anger flared from his eyes. "*You* made this happen. If you'd been a better wife, I wouldn't have had to go to such great lengths to prove myself to you. You killed our girl."

Andi's knees gave out and she crumpled to the ground, wrapping her arms around her middle. She knew what he said was a deranged lie. It didn't stop the pain.

"And now you're going to kill me," she said weakly.

"It's only fair, isn't it? Oh, I stayed for a year, put on a good show for the people, played the supportive and grieving husband and father. But I was done with you after that. You were so far into grieving that I was practically invisible. You were useless to me, so I moved on. Apparently you have, too. I saw you with your cop the other night, getting all cozy at Shelby's. What a joke. Are you sleeping with him, too?"

So he'd been following her and had seen her with Ryan. "You've been following me all along." It explained the constant sense of someone watching her. She didn't bother dignifying his other question with an answer.

"Of course I have," he scoffed.

Andi rose slowly to her feet, bracing her hands along the tree trunk for leverage. He'd followed her. Messed with her head. And he'd assaulted Ryan because of her. It was that last thing that gave her the strength and courage to stand up. Ryan would want her to fight and save herself.

She thought of one of her favorite Bible verses and repeated it in her head.

Be strong and of good courage, do not fear nor be afraid of them; for the LORD your God, He is the One who goes with you. He will not leave you nor forsake you.

Then she looked at Jim, knowing that what she was about to say would set him off but that she needed to say it anyway. For herself. For her daughter.

"I am not yours. I am myself and I am a child of God, but I am not yours."

He was on her in a flash, pinning her to the tree, his hand tight around her neck. "Don't ever say that again."

"Just tell me one thing, Jim," she said, her voice raspy from the choke hold he had on her throat. "Why the rabbit? Why tag the garage and slash my tires and follow me? Why bother, after all this time?"

He smiled then, a ghoulish sort of smile that sent a chill to her bones. "That rabbit has tortured me for seven years. I used it to torture you, of course. So that when I finally kill you, you'll die knowing I was the one pulling all the strings. Because you ruined my life, and now I'm going to ruin yours."

Then he took four steps back, lifted his hand and aimed the gun.

Ryan moved stealthily down the path, keeping as quiet as possible as he approached the clearing. He unclipped his holster and removed his Smith & Wesson.

He'd never had to discharge his sidearm in service before, and he didn't want to today, either, but he'd be ready. He paused and kept his breath quiet, listening intently. There. A man's voice up ahead. Ryan's heart beat out a tattoo and he measured his breathing while he moved forward again, slowly but steadily.

The clearing was just around a bend, and Ryan stepped off the trail, which put him in full view, and cringed as his shoes crunched against dry leaves and twigs. A few more steps and he'd have a good view of the clearing and know what he was dealing with. And pray that his footsteps didn't alert Jim to his presence.

Patience. He had to stay patient, even when everything in him was urging him to hurry.

He took a step and waited, then another, and another. After what felt like a lifetime, he finally got a good look at the clearing and Andi's and Jim's positions. Jim was pacing, and Andi was at the birch tree. His heart leaped as he saw her, from fear and from relief and from…love. There was no mistaking the emotion filling his chest and expanding his heart right now. She had her chin lifted and he couldn't make out what she said to her ex-husband, but it agitated Jim further. Ryan strained to hear what he was saying.

"I only wanted to make her be quiet, don't you see? She just needed to be quiet and sleep a little longer. I didn't mean for it to happen. She ruined the whole plan. And then she just… She stopped breathing."

His lips dropped open. Jim had actually just confessed to killing his own kid. He saw the devastation on Andi's face, heard Jim blame her for everything. Watched her crumple to the ground. He clenched his jaw. Jim was too close to her right now. He had to pick his moment and not go off half-cocked. *Please, Lord, guide my hand today. Stand with me.*

Then, to his surprise, Andi gripped the back of the tree and stood, looking tall and strong and spectacularly unbeaten. She said something and Jim was on her, gun dangling from his hand, his other fingers around her throat. Ryan took a step forward, then another.

"Just tell me one thing, Jim. Why the rabbit? Why tag the garage and slash my tires and follow me? Why bother, after all this time?"

"To torture you, of course. So that when I finally kill you, you'll die knowing I was the one pulling all the strings. Because you ruined my life, and now I'm going to ruin yours."

Jim stood back and lifted the gun, pointing it directly at Andi.

Ryan stepped into the clearing.

"Police! Drop your weapon and get on the ground!"

Chapter Seventeen

Andi jerked her head toward the sound and saw Ryan step through the trees, his gun in his hands, his entire body focused on Jim as Jim spun around in alarm. Her heart slammed into her throat as Ryan paused in a standoff with Jim. "Drop the gun, Jim. Do it now!"

They were in a triangle now, and Andi could see the intensity on Ryan's face as well as the insanity on Jim's. How on earth could he be smiling right now? What had gone so horribly wrong that this was some sort of game to him? "Do as he says, Jim, please!" she pleaded. "No one needs to get hurt today."

Jim turned his head and met her gaze. She didn't recognize the man behind the eyes anymore. Maybe she never had. He kept the smile in place and raised the gun at her. Then in one quick motion, he shifted to point it at Ryan.

A sharp crack echoed in the clearing, followed by a yelp as Jim fell to the ground, his gun landing a few feet away.

Andi dashed forward and kicked it as far as she could so he couldn't reach it again. Ryan, meanwhile, came forward to see to Jim. "Stay down," he barked.

"My arm! You shot me in the arm!"

"Your shoulder, actually, and you'll live," Ryan replied. "Andi?"

She was a nurse, after all. She blinked away the panic at what had just happened and instead focused on Jim's wound. His face was pasty and a sweat had broken out, but a quick assessment showed that the bullet had gone right through. "You're lucky," she said. She reached into her pocket and found a pair of thin knitted gloves. "Best I can do." She pressed one against the wound to help stop the bleeding. "He's going to need to have it cleaned and stitched and some painkillers."

Ryan took twenty seconds to call it in, but it was only another thirty and his backup arrived with an ambulance dispatched to the scene. Ryan stood to the side, letting the other officers take over. His gaze found Andi, and with a cry, she moved forward and into his arms.

They tightened around her with a ferocity that stole her breath. In the moment he'd stepped into the clearing, she'd realized something that shook her to the soles of her feet. She loved Ryan Davenport. The idea that Jim might hurt him had been a knife to her heart. But Ryan hadn't wavered. He'd saved her. Saved her, when for a long time she'd wondered if she was worth saving.

The tears she'd held in for the past hour now slipped down her cheeks. Tears for him, and for her, and for Chelsea; tears that released all the adrenaline coursing through her system and washed away the fear of the last few weeks.

"Shhh," he whispered against her hair. "It's all right. You're all right now."

"He was going to kill me," she whispered. "He hated me that much."

Ryan leaned back and put his hands on her arms. "Andi, Jim has reasons for what he did that have nothing to do with you. When a man hates like that…" He shivered a little. "He made his own choices."

"You shot him. How did you manage to aim for his shoulder?"

He stiffened beneath her hands. "I didn't. No one's that good a shot in the heat of the moment. Someone else was guiding my hand today."

She sniffled and hugged him closer. "I think He was looking out for both of us."

She could hear Jim sobbing now in the clearing. "I didn't mean to kill her. She was my baby. She wouldn't stop crying. I needed her to stop crying. I just tried to stop her from crying…"

"I can't listen to that any longer," she said, turning away, her heart breaking for what felt like the millionth time. For years she'd wanted to catch Chelsea's killer. Never had she expected the victory to feel this horrible and empty.

"I can't leave, not yet. You need to be checked out, too." He motioned to one of the other officers, a woman. "Constable Brown, can you take Ms. Wallace to the hospital to be checked out?"

Andi shook her head. "No! I want to stay with you."

He put his hand along the side of her face. It was firm and warm and made her feel so safe. "Andi, this is an active crime scene, and I discharged my weapon. Those are things I need to deal with right now. But I promise, the moment I can, I'll come find you, okay? Constable Brown will take you to be checked, and, sweetheart, you're going to need to talk to someone. You've had a significant trauma."

She picked out the word *sweetheart* and relaxed just a little. "You'll find me?"

He nodded, and to her surprise, she saw tears in his eyes. "I'll always find you, okay?"

Her lower lip wobbled as she nodded. "Okay." She turned to look at the constable and took a breath. "Okay."

But as they reached the edge of the clearing, Andi turned and looked back. "Just a moment," she said, turning away from Constable Brown. She stood there, looking at the circle where her life had changed forever. Now, though, maybe there would be justice. Her gaze fell on Ryan, and a warmth filled her chest. And maybe, for her, a new beginning.

Andi woke early the next morning, even before the sun rose. It was Thanksgiving Sunday, and yet the day ahead felt so surreal. There was so much to process. So much to unravel. She put on a pot of coffee and then wrapped herself in a warm shawl and went out on the back porch with a mug of steaming brew.

A magpie strutted through the grass, his long tail behind him, and Andi sank into her porch chair. The sky was turning a paler shade of periwinkle, with a blazing pink streak where the sun would soon appear. It was a day like any other day, but a day after which nothing would be the same.

Could she go through with today? The thought of a big Davenport holiday meal seemed overwhelming. She sipped the coffee and let out a long, slow breath. It was over. She had to let it be over. And yet…

She'd thought justice would bring closure. That somehow knowing Chelsea's killer was behind bars would make it hurt less. She was just now discovering it didn't hurt less. It just meant there were other complicated feelings to sort through.

The crunch of gravel announced a car in her driveway, and she turned to see Shelby's minivan. Her throat tightened. She'd been so tired last night that she'd collapsed in bed and fallen into a fitful slumber. She hadn't called Shelby. She'd managed one call to her parents to tell them the news before they saw it on TV or online. And Ryan had done what he'd promised. He'd found her at the detachment, giving her statement. Her car was still being searched for evidence, so when she was done he drove her home, but he hadn't come in. It had hurt a little, but she thought she understood. Yesterday had been a lot, all the way around.

Shelby got out and walked up the steps, took one look at Andi and went inside. She came out moments later with her own cup of coffee and sat down on the other side of the porch chair. Still, she said nothing. She just sat there, keeping Andi company, drinking coffee, while they watched the miracle of the dawn.

Finally, Andi cradled her cup and said, "I'm in love with your brother."

Shelby took a drink. "Does he know that?"

"No."

Shelby turned her head and looked at Andi. "Are you going to tell him?"

"I don't know." Andi met her friend's gaze. "There's a lot to sort through. And maybe he doesn't feel the same."

Finally, Shelby's face relaxed and she smiled. "Sweetie, I guarantee he feels the same. I've never seen him act around anyone the way he acts around you."

"Jim said he knocked Ryan out on Friday."

"He did. Gave him a big goose egg on the back of his head. Even so, he went into work and spent the whole day chasing down leads again." She reached over and patted Andi's hand. "He didn't tell me what, but last night he said that even if Jim hadn't kidnapped you, they had new evidence against him. He was so determined to solve that case."

But Andi knew Ryan was just doing his job. That didn't mean he loved her. "I have so many things going on in my head. What guy would want to take that on?"

Shelby leaned over and looked into Andi's eyes. "He told me he kissed you. Andi, nothing has to be decided today. And you had all that baggage before yesterday. He still cared for you. Give him the benefit of the doubt. He's a good man, even if he is my little brother."

Andi smiled. "When I saw him coming through the trees yesterday, it was like everything fell into place. I always said I never wanted to be rescued, but I needed him and he was there. He has been there ever since I called him the day I found that rabbit nailed to the tree."

Shelby's gaze darkened. "Jim is a sick so-and-so to do something like that."

"I've been thinking about it. I haven't been able to stop thinking about it, actually. I knew he had a bad childhood, but maybe it was worse than I thought. Maybe it all started with some sort of trauma. Or maybe he has some sort of brain imbalance…"

Shelby shook her head. "Honey, that's not for you to figure out. You'll go around and around in circles trying to figure out why people do the awful things they do."

"That's what Ryan said."

Again, Shelby smiled. "I'm going to be honest. Ryan slept at our place last night. He didn't want to go home. He's pretty shaken, though he wouldn't say so. I don't think he's ever actually had to fire his weapon in all the years he's served. I think seeing you in danger affected him, too. You need to see each other. To talk about it."

"I'm not sure I'm up to Thanksgiving dinner today," Andi admitted.

"We have a lot to be thankful for this year," Shelby replied, sitting back and taking a big drink of her coffee once more. "You're safe. Chelsea's case is solved. We're all healthy and have roofs over our heads. Seems to me having some turkey and pie is a good way to celebrate all that."

Shelby was right. And Andi knew she had to leave her house or else she'd risk falling into the same trap she did when Chelsea died: keeping to herself too much. "Just don't expect a miracle," she advised.

"We've already had one." Shelby's voice thickened with emotion. "You're sitting here safe and sound. I would be lost without my best friend. And that's true whether you and Ryan make a go of things or not."

Andi's throat thickened and she reached over and took Shelby's hand. Maybe it was time she let go of some of the pain and started being thankful.

Shelby and family went back to pick up Andi to take her to dinner, since her car still hadn't been returned. Andi stepped out at Mr. and Mrs. Davenport's and immediately smelled what was sure to be a tasty dinner: the roasting scent of turkey, sage, and also cinnamon and cloves. The Davenport home was decorated in fine fashion for Thanksgiving. Pumpkins lined the front steps of the two-story house nestled among trees that desperately clung to their leaves in a final show of color. There was a wreath in autumn colors on the front door, and when Andi got inside, the smells intensified. Her stomach growled. She'd barely eaten since yesterday, but perhaps she could do justice to this dinner.

"We're here!" Shelby called out, then immediately started instructing kids to take off their shoes and put them neatly on the mat, hang up their coats, and not to run. The first two tasks were done well, but the third was abandoned as Shelby's mom appeared from the kitchen and held out her arms. Then her two oldest grandchildren broke into a run for hugs.

Andi smiled, feeling a wistfulness at the scene before her. She was so pleased to be included, but it was bittersweet, too.

Ryan appeared in the doorway, his gaze somber as it met hers.

Then tears pricked the backs of her lids and she stepped forward, and he did, too, and within seconds he'd enveloped her in a hug. "I'm so glad you're okay," he whispered, giving her a squeeze, then stepping back.

She was aware the family had discreetly disappeared, and her cheeks heated. "I'm sorry. It's just... I haven't seen you since yesterday and I'm glad you're okay, too."

"I was going to come by last night but thought it might be too late." His stormy eyes searched hers. "And I thought maybe you wouldn't want me to."

"Why wouldn't I want you to?" She frowned.

"I—" He started to speak but then broke off. "Listen, dinner isn't for another half hour. Do you want to go for a walk?"

"I was going to help in the kitchen..."

"I think they'll understand. My mother would shoo you away, anyway."

She nodded. "All right, then. Let me put my jacket back on."

They stepped out into the crisp fall day, and Ryan reached down to take her hand. "Is this okay?" he asked.

It was more than okay. "It's fine," she replied, trying to make sense of everything running through her head and heart and not knowing exactly where to start.

They walked through the backyard toward his parents' vegetable garden, now empty except for some pumpkin and squash vines. Off to the side was a smaller flower garden, with a couple of bird feeders hanging up and a bench beside it. It was the bench they gravitated to, and they sat on the weathered wood.

"Jim confessed last night. To everything." Ryan turned to face her. "Some of our working theories were right. He did access the site from the old logging road, and you were right about him using the walking trail to get into your yard." He let out a big breath. "On Friday, I got a lead that he'd had his car repaired at a body shop in Red Deer right after you'd almost been run off the road. And we found a link between him and the scene in the woods on the day of Chelsea's death. For what it's worth, his plan was twisted and sick, but I believe he never meant to kill her."

"He just wanted my attention. All of my attention," she said bitterly.

"Even if he hadn't confessed, we would have had him on the kidnapping charge, weapons offenses. He's not licensed to have a handgun, so he came by it illegally. He's not going to bother you ever again, Andi."

She nodded, feeling both relief and sadness. "I wish I understood why."

"You might not. Not ever. And that's okay. I'm not sure it's ever understandable when someone does what he did." He sighed. "That's between him and God now."

Her annoyance flared. "Is it that easy?" she asked. "Forgiveness? Because I'm not sure I can ever do that."

"You have every right to be angry," he stated. "I'm angry. But you don't have to go through this alone. All I know is that hate is a poison that eats at you from the inside out. Forgiveness is where the healing is."

She knew he was right. It was a lot to ask today. But

maybe someday… "I don't want to live my life being angry all the time," she murmured. "I want to move on. I want to…actually have a life. I'm so tired of it all being so heavy. Ryan, there's something else you should know. I was going to tell you yesterday, and it's why I texted you. Jim…he had a thing with our babysitter."

He didn't look surprised. She stared at him. "You knew."

"I heard a rumor, but I couldn't say anything to you until it was confirmed. Everything moved too quickly after that. I got hit on the head. Then Ben and I chased down leads all day, and yesterday morning we tried to find Jim for questioning."

"He got her pregnant."

"I'm sorry, Andi."

"Me, too, but I'm more sorry for Leslie. She told me everything yesterday, and she's really struggling. He's caused havoc in so many lives. But I forgive her. It'll take me longer with Jim. If ever."

Ryan was quiet for a moment, and when she looked over at him, he looked uncomfortable. This was the moment, she realized. The moment where he was going to say they could just be friends. That they'd got close because of the case, but it was over now.

She wished she could think of something to keep him from saying it, but her brain blanked.

"Andi, listen. It's going to take a while for this case to be resolved, though with a full confession it'll be shorter than most. Even so, I could be in huge trouble if you and I are involved while this is still ongoing."

Here it comes, she thought, and steeled herself for the letdown.

"But I care about you, Andi. So much. It's been awful, trying to keep my feelings to myself and pretending to be the cop and best friend's helpful brother. I want so much more. And I know this is rotten timing, so I guess what I'm asking is…will you wait for me?"

Her mouth dropped open in surprise as she stared at him. "Wait…for you?"

He nodded. "Once this is settled, I'd like to take you out. On a real date. Not the diner as a thank-you or a sandwich for helping you scrub off graffiti. I mean dress up and go out on an actual date."

The tiny seed of hope she'd been burying to avoid disappointment suddenly bloomed. "Ryan, I—"

He cut her off again, but she didn't mind because he seemed to need to get things off his chest. "It would give us time, too, to deal with what happened. I'm going to be honest, Andi. I was pretty traumatized the first time I was at that clearing in the woods. Seeing you there, your life in danger… I'm going to need some help working through that. And you have your own trauma. I want to give us space to do that, to start to heal…but I also want you to know that when we're ready, I want to be there for you. Not as Shelby's brother but as a…as a…"

He couldn't seem to find the right word, but she didn't care. He was so considerate, so principled. She loved that about him. And despite all the disillusionment about her first marriage, she held none of those concerns about Ryan. She couldn't project Jim's behavior on men in general. Especially a man like Ryan, who was so caring and giving.

"I would love to go on a real date with you," she said softly.

"You mean it."

"Yes, of course I mean it." She reached over and linked her hand with his again. "You're absolutely right about how we both need to start healing from this. But over the past few weeks I've developed feelings for you, too, Ryan. Ones I didn't expect to have again. So yes. When you're free to ask me, my answer will be yes."

His eyes lit up as a smile bloomed on his face. "That's really good news," he said. "The best."

"We have a lot to be thankful for." She ran her thumb over his hand. "Including each other. Now, let's go inside and eat that amazing-smelling dinner your mom has made."

They got up from the bench, but Ryan hesitated a moment, before stepping forward and dropping a soft kiss on her forehead. "It's my turn to say grace this year," he murmured. "And I know exactly what I'm thankful for."

Chapter Eighteen

Eleven months later

Andi got out of the car and straightened her sweater, then reached behind her for the bundle of daisies tied with ribbon the color of sunshine. Ryan got out of the driver's side and sent her a smile before coming around the car and taking her hand.

"Ready?" he asked.

She nodded. "Ready."

It was September 19, but this year Andi wasn't going back into the woods to talk to Chelsea. Instead, she was here, at the cemetery next to the church, to visit her little girl's gravestone. There was a peace that came from closing the case and starting to heal. The past months had been full of legalities, certainly, but also of counseling and therapy and, most of all, faith. Jim was in prison and would remain there. Partially thanks to Caroline's testimony, it was determined that the end of his relationship with her had caused him to have a "break." The details of his crimes had been tough to face, but Andi had done it, with her parents and Shelby by her side and with Ryan there in his capacity as an officer and as a friend.

She looked up at him now and smiled, and he smiled back. It was impossible to believe he hadn't been placed into her life for a reason.

The leaves were changing on the trees surrounding the church, and along the fence, goldenrod and Queen Anne's lace sent off a warm, fall-ish aroma. Together they walked through the cemetery until they arrived at the small stone marker.

Andi stepped forward. "Hello, sweetheart," she said softly, and knelt to place the daisies at the base of the stone. "I miss you."

Pain settled at the pit of her stomach—pain she now realized would never go away. But it was different somehow. It wasn't that Andi was ready to let her go. It was more that Andi was ready to open her life to more. Chelsea would always be in her heart and a part of her story. But for the first time, she felt as if she still had a life to live that was not defined by the death of her daughter.

She looked over her shoulder at Ryan. It was all because of him. She held out her hand and he took it, helping her up. Andi brushed the dried grass off her knees and then straightened. "Let's walk," she said.

They ambled through the gate of the cemetery and then around the church grounds. Mums and dahlias bloomed, the last vestiges of the flower gardens, and the lawn was starting to turn brown; the summer had been a dry one. Behind the parking lot was an open area with several picnic tables, which congregants used for outdoor events or after-service get-togethers. Shelby's kids had spent time here in the summer during Vacation Bible School, doing crafts on the wooden tables and eating bagged lunches. Andi leaned against one and ran her hand over the top. "'God is our refuge and strength, a very present help in trouble,'" she quoted. She smiled at Ryan. "I know I told you this before, but when Chelsea died, I lost my faith. Now, though… I don't know how I would have got through the last year without it." She squeezed his fingers. "And without you. I truly believe He sent you to me."

Ryan was quiet for a few moments, and then he reached into his pocket. "Andi, I love you. You know I do. I didn't really think I wanted the whole marriage and family thing until you. I do want those things. I want them with you. But only if you want them, too." His gaze delved into hers. "Losing Chelsea was so hard. And clearly your marriage has left its mark." His jaw tightened. "I understand if you don't want those things. If it…hurts too much."

Andi smiled then, so incredibly happy that she was sure she must glow with it, as if a candle had been lit inside her. "You want a family. Babies."

He nodded. "I want it all. But if you don't, I mean…" He closed his eyes and sighed. "I'm messing this up."

"You're doing fine," she said, as the butterflies in her stomach took flight.

That seemed to reassure him, because he smiled. "The truth is, Andi, I love you. I want you with me, whether there are babies or not. If you want them, you've got 'em.

If you don't, well, that's fine, too. It won't make me love you less or—" he picked up her left hand "—want to be married to you any less."

She looked down and saw he held a diamond ring.

"Will you marry me, Andi?"

It had been a long road to get here. There'd been joy but so much pain. Why would she ever refuse the chance to have that joy again? "I fell in love with you the day you first kissed me on your sister's step," she admitted. "I know we needed to take our time, but I also hoped it would lead us to this moment." And it was the perfect moment. Today she'd made a monumental step toward living in the present rather than the past. "Yes, I'll marry you, right here in this church, in front of our families and friends. And yes, I want babies." Tears gathered on her lashes and slipped down her cheeks. "I loved being a mother. I want to do that again, with you."

He slid the ring over her finger, then cupped her face in his hands. "I love you forever," he said. And as he nestled her in his arms, and she could hear his heartbeat against her ear, she thanked God for her own little miracle and a second chance at happiness.

* * * * *

LOVE INSPIRED

Stories to uplift and inspire

Fall in love with Love Inspired—
inspirational and uplifting stories of faith
and hope. Find strength and comfort in
the bonds of friendship and community.
Revel in the warmth of possibility and the
promise of new beginnings.

Sign up for the Love Inspired newsletter
at **LoveInspired.com** to be the first
to find out about upcoming titles,
special promotions and exclusive content.

CONNECT WITH US AT:

f Facebook.com/LoveInspiredBooks

🐦 Twitter.com/LoveInspiredBks

SPECIAL EXCERPT FROM

❧

LOVE INSPIRED SUSPENSE
INSPIRATIONAL ROMANCE

*Searching for her best friend's remains could help
forensic anthropologist Melanie Hutton regain her
memories of when they were both kidnapped—and
put her right back in the killer's sights. But can
Detective Jason Cooper set the past aside to help her
solve his sister's murder…and shield Melanie from
the same fate?*

Read on for a sneak peek at
Buried Cold Case Secrets,
a new Love Inspired Suspense story by Sami A. Abrams!

Melanie wiped her hand down her face. "Jason. We're going
to be working together for the foreseeable future. Do you
think we can call a truce at least while we do our jobs?"

His jaw twitched, and he remained silent.

She'd asked a lot, but the strain between them had to stop.
She watched him for a few minutes then shook her head.

"Never mind." She pushed from the trunk and limped to
the hole in the ground. Her lead-filled heart threatened to
drop to her feet. To think that fifteen years ago she'd had a
crush on him. If only she could return to those carefree days.
The days before she had died on the inside and her friend
had died for real.

Someday, Allison, I'll find your body. I promise.

She swiped the wetness from her cheeks and lowered
herself into the grave. The movement mimicked her mood.
She picked up her trowel and searched for more bones.

An hour later, Melanie's headache had become unbearable, causing her stomach to roil. Scanning the grave, she spotted the paintbrush she used for delicate work. She grasped the handle but dropped it. She tried again, but her fingers refused to cooperate. Her eyelids grew heavy. Something was off. She sat on the edge of the hole.

"Jason, help." Her words were slurred. She struggled to stay upright. The trees in front of her blurred and swayed.

He kneeled down and came face-to-face with her. "What's wrong?"

"I don't know."

"Help me out here. What's the last thing you did?"

"I—I…" She struggled against the gray cloud jumbling her thoughts. "Took a break a while ago. Only digging since."

His gaze flew to a spot behind her.

She wilted into him. Her vision tunneled, and darkness closed in.

"Keith! Grab the cooler and her bag!"

Jason's frantic voice registered, but her body had shut down.

His warm arms lifted her.

Her cheek bounced against his chest in cadence with the pounding of his feet on the path.

His rhythmic breathing was the last thing she heard before the world went dark.

Don't miss
Buried Cold Case Secrets *by Sami A. Abrams,*
available January 2022 wherever
Love Inspired Suspense books and ebooks are sold.

LoveInspired.com

IF YOU ENJOYED THIS BOOK
WE THINK YOU WILL ALSO LOVE

LOVE INSPIRED
INSPIRATIONAL ROMANCE
MOUNTAIN RESCUE

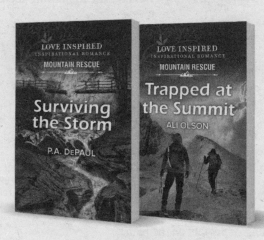

Courage. Danger. Faith.

Find strength and determination in stories
of faith and love in the face of danger.

AVAILABLE JANUARY 25, 2022

LIMRBPA1221

SPECIAL EXCERPT FROM

LOVE INSPIRED
INSPIRATIONAL ROMANCE

MOUNTAIN RESCUE

Pouring rain, a rising river...and two missing teens.

Can Nathan Porter and Reena Wells put aside their differences and find the teens...before tragedy strikes on the mountain?

Read on for a sneak preview of
Surviving the Storm,
a new Love Inspired Mountain Rescue story by P.A. DePaul!

"Listen up, everyone." Reena Wells raised her voice to compete with the group of teens and chaperones forming a loose circle in the dirt clearing. "We've made it to the second stop on our hike for the day, so that means—"

"Scavenger hunt!"

Reena laughed. "And here I thought you'd be groaning to nap after this last stretch of uphill climb or complaining about the lack of cell phone signal."

"You haven't been listening to my uncle, then," Ashleigh Porter joked dryly, thumbing toward the good-looking man beside her, towering over her by a foot.

Said uncle scowled at his niece. "Et tu, Brute?"

Ashleigh rolled her eyes. "No Shakespeare during summer break. It's a rule."

Nathan Porter dropped a tanned arm over Ashleigh's shoulders and pulled his niece in for a side hug. Her gaze flicked to the ground, but Reena caught the slice of pain in her eyes. A small pang twisted Reena's heart at the tragedy the fifteen-year-old had suffered six months ago. Never knowing her mother, who died during childbirth, was already tough, but losing her father in a freak construction accident was horrible.

"All righty." Reena handed out a sheaf of green papers. "Here are the items to find. Remember, only pictures on your cell phones are needed as proof. We're not out to damage the environment."

"How much interaction are chaperones allowed to have in the search?" Nathan asked.

"None," Reena answered.

Nathan's dark brown eyes narrowed. "None as in no pointing out items or—"

"None as in chaperones aren't going out with the teams."

"But it's dangerous in the forest," Nathan cut in. "Someone could get lost or hurt."

"True," Reena said. "But kids need to learn how to handle those situations without an adult swooping in and doing everything for them. Besides—" she rushed to head off Nathan's next protest "—it's a small search area and I've included a map. Everyone will be fine. We have to trust the teens are old enough and intelligent enough to handle a simple scavenger hunt."

"Uncle Nathan," Ashleigh hissed. "I'll be fine."

Nathan scratched the scruff adorning his jawline, then nodded. "Okay."

Ashleigh blew out an audible breath while Reena exhaled as silently as she could. "You've got forty-five minutes to return back here, whether you find everything or not." Raising her arm, Reena shouted, "Happy hunting!"

The presence of a dark cloud slowly blotting out the sun couldn't be ominous or a harbinger in any way, right?

Don't miss
Surviving the Storm *by P.A. DePaul,*
available February 2022
wherever Love Inspired books and ebooks are sold.

LoveInspired.com

LIMREXP1221